IMAGINE:

A Wild Civilisation

by

CHARLIE BATT

IMAGINE Series: Book 1

This book is a work of fiction. Names, characters, places, magazine and incidents are the product of the author's imagination or are used fictitiously. Any resemblance to actual events, locales, or persons, living or dead, is coincidental.

ISBN 978-0-6452232-1-7

About Charlie

Charlie Batt lives on the east coast of Australia. She is a very talented fourteen-year-old who is on the autism spectrum. She loves storytelling and drawing and has put her talents into writing the Imagine series.

Book 1. Imagine: A Wild Civilization

Book 2. Imagine: A Long Winter

Book 3. Imagine: The Golden Starpearl

Book 4. Imagine: High Worlds

Book 5. Imagine: A Dark Underworld

COLOUR CODES OF CHARACTERS

GREEN-Stephenie

PINK - Charlie

DARK BLUE - Bucky

RED - Hajuan

LIGHT GREY - Monster Minions

ORANGE - Violet

LIGHT RED - Chuckboi

BLUE -Tar

DARK BLUE - Sandy

PINK, BLUE and RED - Atom

DARK GREEN - Eric

MIXED - two or more characters

DARK PURPLE - The Sorcerer

DARK RED - Scarlet

DARK BLUE - Scarlet's two trusted Royal Guards

Light blue - The Sorcerer's demons

PURPLE AND RED - Corrupted Sorcerer

DARKISH RED - Monster Archers

LIGHT DARK BLUE - Ching Ching

PROLOGUE

Tomorrow was Christmas.

It wasn't long away, and I was really excited! Probably more excited than my nine best friends: Chuckboi—his real name is Chuck, but I like to call him Chuckboi—Stephenie, Atom, Eric, Tar, Violet, Sandy, Barbara and Bucky. It's our favourite time of the year! We put up the Christmas tree on our ship, known as the Alphanian Ship, and helped the Pollen villagers too.

Pollen Village is just across from the forest that surrounds our ship's home. The name, Pollen Village comes from all the flowers huddling the houses, the farms, merchants' stores and the school that sit in the centre of the Green Plains. Our Alphanian Ship by the way, is huge and even though it looks like it's small on the outside, it's bigger inside.

Strange, right? It has everything and every room that we are mindful of. With large sails like other ships that you know, it even has the pattern of my Mindatar symbols. The symbols on my forehead are like eyes the other way around and round eyelashes on each side, and no, the symbol is not a tattoo.

Anyway, we celebrate the joy with each other, and as Alphanians we create fireworks with the fire dust I summon. We make our own fire stars. When we're done, I bring them together, bind them, then shoot them up to the night sky. We watch as they fly and spread joy all around Hybrainia.

We were so full of joy, we even had Christmas parties on Christmas Eve. Tar is our Music Master and the Alpha of Music, and to admit, he's incredible at DJing.

"Oh my goodness, I am *so* excited! Aren't you guys?" I said to everyone as we finally headed to the Den, the place in the ship where we sleep.

"Very!" my pal, Bucky said, looking at me with a huge smile on his face. Bucky is a young Gippyguppy, a kind of salamander, and so is Barbara, and they are the smallest and youngest

8

Alphas in our team. Bucky is yellow and has an amethyst Amulet on the thick purple tip of his forehead. He and Barbara both have long but different tails that show their gender. Bucky has yellow eyes, with a teal iris and black pupils. He also has two bright teal axolotl gills on each side of his eyes and fins too. His two legs have two dark blue stripes—Gippyguppies, in fact, can walk on two or all four.

Barbara on the other hand is a female Gippyguppy, but her smooth skin is light blue. She has only one small round dark blue fin on each side of her face. Her eyes are big and a beautiful light blue iris and she wears a necklace made out of pearls and a little gold circle with a heart in the middle—the pearls are technically her Amulet, but the gold she touches in the front makes them glow.

She is a year younger than Bucky, and has no stripes and her tail is full of dark blue.

We reached the Den eventually, and settled ourselves down on our spots. Usually Bucky and

Chuckboi rest between me. Sandy and Barbara sleep with each other, as do Eric, Violet, Tar and Stephenie. But Atom just sleeps by himself, which he doesn't mind at all.

Speaking of Atom, he's named that because he is basically made out of a gigantic group of atoms and merged. He grew white arms and green legs. His head is an oxygen atom and his body is made of other atoms connected to each other. When he grew his arms and legs, they had no fingers or toes, so Atom is fingerless and toeless. He wears his red lab goggles that he never takes off his head. He loves science, mathematics, experiments and data that he collects whenever we go on our adventures, and he is still learning about our world. He also has a sapphire Amulet like me, but his is shaped like a question mark. It also has special wires connected to it and the gold base straps onto his yellow belly.

"Char'i," Stephenie said to me using the Japanese version of my name. Stephenie is a green Alpha Singanoid with central heterochromia. Which means she has two colours in her eyes. She has orange and pink within each eye and clean lime skin. Her hair is orange with a round crimson fringe that has a curl on her right side of her face. She also has two little blue tips sticking out from under her fringe. Three pink spots sit under each of her eyes and there are two yellow curls on her forehead. Between them is her diamond Amulet shaped like a medic symbol, but pointier. She wears a light blue robe that has two longer yellow curls with two pink lines between a lime heart in the centre of her robe.

By the way, she calls me 'Char'i' because I used to tell her how I said my name in Japanese when we were younger. I don't really mind her calling me that.

"Yeah, Steph?" I said.

"I cannot believe how far we went this year," she replied.

"Yeah. I was hoping we would."

"Why?" she asked.

"Because I wanted to see my best friend,

11

Jundamir when he reaches high school."

"Oh," she said.

"We did have fun together," Chuckboi said. Chuckboi is a Dragadillo. He is red and bigger than all of us with a brown shell that is as solid as stone on his back and up his head. His shell has two big chubby points between each side and small points between the sides of his head. He has a long prehensile tail for grabbing and holding things. He has brown magical eyes and sharper teeth than we do, because he is particularly a dragon. He wears a gold collar with an emerald Amulet on the front. Iron bands circle his legs and gold blades sit on his shoulders.

"And sang," Tar added. Tar is an Alpha Singanoid like Stephenie, but he's blue and with heterochromia eyes, swirling colours on the curls from down his cheeks and above his eyes. He has a red round logo above his left eye with a lightning bolt on it. He wears a robe of many colours and has an opal Amulet on his gold collar. His hair is teal with a white fringe and there are pink, purple and yellow points on each side of his fringe.

"And explored," said Sandy. Sandy is a Batfish. She is blue and has sharp greyish blue spines that are as sharp as needles on her head. Two large dark blue spots sit between the sides of her head; her main ones are bigger and the ones beside them are smaller. She has two aquatic wings with her long thin arms connected to them, a big tail for swimming smoothly and quickly, and tiny legs for her to walk on land. She has an aquamarine Amulet on her forehead and a golden band on each of her arms with aquatic stones in each. She has big eyes and two pupils on each one, two big ones and two small ones.

"We've done hundreds of things this year. And hopefully we can do it again next year," Violet said while her bells jingled on her three tall orange horns on her head. Violet is small except the three large orange horns on the top of her head—Horns is also her last name. The front horn has a peridot Amulet that is shaped like a love heart with a yellow base behind it. She wears orange armour

13

with two dark blue collars on top and bottom. She also wears green pants like I do. Her irises are as green as her Amulet. Because she hangs out with tar mostly, she wanted eyelashes. So Tar painted some under her eyes and carefully around her triangles under her eyes. That tells her gender; if it's a male, they have one but if it's a female, they have two.

"I need to admit, it has been a little tough in the human world because of COVID. Good thing is, we all managed to survive the whole year without getting infected," I said to everyone.

"It has been a tough year, but the human doctors are working on a vaccine to stop it," Eric replied. He is a reptile like Violet and Chuckboi, but a little between them in their height. He is a Chamilio Lozard which is a type of chameleon in Hybrainia. He is faster than the fastest animal on Earth. He has green scaly skin and changes colour depending on his feelings. For example: if he feels scared, he'll turn white or if he's feeling guilty, he'll turn orange. He has three tails with unique patterns on each. He wears a dark blue metallic brace on his middle tail with a turquoise Amulet. Like Chuckboi, he and Violet also have sharp teeth, but not the sharpest.

"I know," I said, smiling. "Now, we should all rest and get ready for tomorrow."

"We should," Bucky agreed and lay down comfortably next to me, resting his sleepy teal eyes. We said goodnight and Merry Christmas to each other, and all rested our eyes, ready for the special day tomorrow: Christmas Day.

Chapter 1

A brand-new day and another year!

Christmas was SO much fun last year! We all got gifts from each other. I got a lot of arts and crafts stuff.

Stephenie got a blue orchid from Tar (which is one of my favourite colours).

Atom has things that he can study and experiment with, like scales, plants, materials and other things.

We visited Pollen Village for lunch. We had chicken that had homemade soy (Chuckboi, Violet and Eric can't eat soy because it would make them sick). We even had homemade bread from Farmer Brenda, she makes very good bread from the wheat she grows.

We chatted with the Singanoid villagers and they told us that Bruce, the blacksmith, got a new anvil because the last one seemed pretty damaged after forging and hammering metal, steel and aluminium. Will, the librarian, got new empty books, ready to be written with his stories and research, and Farmer Brenda got better fertiliser for her farm.

The next day came eventually, and we did our usual things.

Atom was studying a kind of antidote called Iemunity. It's a swirling blue glowing medicine, very useful to cure your body from harmful effects, sickness, even infected wounds. Iemunity needs a few ingredients: blue orchids, luminesap, water and leviathan scale powder of any kind. We only harvest their scales when they're dead and if the Singanoids could collect enough until they need to go back up to the surface. I never really went on the water actually.

Stephenie meditated on the hills nearby the Oceanic Mountainside with her orchid that Tar gave her for Christmas. Sandy and Barbara explored the Kelp Forest. Violet, Eric and Tar jammed with his new speakers as he made beats and rhythm. Chuckboi and Bucky chilled outside, and I was going to try new art stuff. But then I stopped for a second before I even touched it, and stared at the window facing east and wondered what was out there.

We had never been east of the ocean. But we have heard from the Singanoids that going east was restrictively forbidden for a reason: sailors have gone east and they never came back, ever. I didn't know what to do. I needed to decide whether to tell my friends, or risk it.

But I'd think about it first.

Chapter 2

The argument about Charlie's decision

I eventually thought of what to do: tell my friends. They'd think I'm insane for what I was doing, but I really, really wanted to do it. I touched the sapphire Amulet on my chestplate and said, "Everyone, I need to tell you all something. Please meet me in the Den tonight."

When night time quickly came eventually, we were grouped together in the Den. I went in front of the group in the back of the room that was filled with the most pillows and we sat our butts down near each other.

I cleared my throat, "Everyone..." I began. "You might think I'm crazy...um..." I hesitated. Everyone was watching me, listening. I struggled to find my words, I was nervous, but too eager to tell them. Stephenie could understand that I was struggling. She came to me, sat next to me and told me to breathe. That helped, I did what she told me, and I finally said, "You may think I'm insane.

But I want to risk the East."

Everyone was shocked when I said that, even Stephenie.

"Charlie, are you out of your Youth?!" Tar exclaimed. (My youth is a legendary plant that allows me to create life)

"That's too dangerous!" Violet shouted worriedly. "Charlie, we are *not* letting you go to the East. It's forbidden."

"But I want to face it. We never went East on the ocean before."

"You're *not* going!" Chuckboi said, getting serious. He gets very tough to be understood when he's serious, but I try to be serious too. Sometimes it's not easy.

"Well, I want to!" I said to him with a look.

"Charlie, *listen!*" Chuckboi yelled, and then there was silence. He got up and towered above me and he shouted. "*None of us are going, and you're not either!*"

My face boiled with anger and I yelled back at him. "*You can't keep me here forever! I'm the leader and the Mindatar!*"

"*We're trying to protect you! And we're against this idea of you going to the east!*"

Chuckboi and I ferociously growled at each other until suddenly, someone shouted, "I'll go!"

We stopped growling and stared at each other, confused. Then we turned and looked at the person who said it. That person walked out of the group and we were surprised.

"Bucky?" we both said at the same time.

"I'll go," he said again. Me, Chuckboi and the others were surprised at Bucky. We had never seen him that brave before.

"Charlie's right," Bucky said.

"I am?" I wondered.

"She is the Mindatar of Hybrainia. She made this world and all of us. She has an adventurous spirit to explore and uncover things she never knew existed. Charlie's immortal. Immortals never die. If she's wanting to explore somewhere new, this is why I'll go," Bucky said persuasively, and shot a smile at me.

I was completely amazed. Persuading everyone on his own? Holy cow he was a brave Gippyguppy! I came past Chuckboi and towards Bucky, and kneeled down to his head level. "That was incredible buddy, pound it," I said to him, I closed my fist and showed it to Bucky, he accepted the fist-bump.

"Bakki? Char'i?" Stephenie asked us.

We both looked at her.

"If you two are going, we'll stay here and wish you good luck. Just be careful out there," she told us, looking worried.

"We will, Steph," I said to her with a smile.

Chapter 3

The big news

The Alphanians had to agree with Charlie, but they didn't know that they weren't alone. A grey Singanoid with red eyes and white pupils was peeking in one of the small round windows on the left side of the Den and he collected all of Charlie's information. Then he carefully climbed down from the side and ran for the Fortress of the Fire Queen. When he got there eventually, he ran from chambers, through hallways and straight to the Throne room, where the information would be told.

"Your Highness!" the Monster said. The Monsters were Singanoids who had their colours taken away by Charlie's Nemesis who was named Scarlet, the Fire Queen. She looked very familiar to Charlie, except she wore a black robe and her hair was fire with a black fringe from one side of her hair and sliding down over her left eye. Her skin was darker than Charlie's.

Scarlet woke up and her flaming hair glowed red and she glared at him. She held her staff with an orange gem shaped like a flame.

"I apologise for waking you up from your slumber, but I have very important news for you."

"Tell me," she said to the Monster, still glaring at him. Her voice was a little deeper than Charlie's.

"The Diamond Alpha is heading to the Eastern side of the ocean to explore," he explained.

Scarlet's right eye widened with surprise. "Tell me more," she said to him, curious.

"The Alphanians gathered on the ship and she told them she was going to the East. But her friends were against it except her little pal. What is your plan, your Majesty?" he asked her.

Scarlet thought about it and tried to hatch a plan. *Heading East for any reason? She must be crazy. Or maybe… she must be going East to find secrets. Yes! She must be doing that.*

24

"We must follow them. Tell the Monster Archer Captain," she commanded him.

"Yes, your Highness?" he said with a confused look, then left the Throne Room.

She knew what he was thinking: 'But your Highness. The East is very dangerous because of storms and creatures lurking below the sea!'

She didn't care at all! All she cared about was discovering secrets before Charlie and Bucky did. She got up from her throne and went through the Crimson Hallway. Her two trusted Royal Guards, who guarded the Throne Room's entrance, guided her to a large veranda high up in the Fortress. Her Royal Guards wore black armour and helmets with two sharp points covered in gold on the tips. They held maces that were sharp and they looked like twins.

When they reached the veranda, Scarlet came to the edge and watched from above. She saw the Monster she had commanded running from the entrance straight to the Captain. The Captain saw him and the Monster told him her

25

orders. Eventually the Captain gave directions to the others. They all followed, and lined up with their backs straight. Scarlet climbed on the veranda.

"Not again," the trusted Royal Guard on the left said quietly, rubbing his eyes.

She sharply turned her head. "What did you say?"

"Oh! Uh … nothing, your Majesty," the Royal Guard on the left said quickly.

She rolled her scarred eye and looked back at the Monsters below and said quietly, "Ugh, idiots." She took off from the ledge and hovered slowly to the ground and then she walked with her staff towards the Monsters. "The Diamond Alpha and her sidekick are heading East of the ocean," she began. "We'll never know what they'll find. So, I have a plan. I need to see a Monster who can navigate through the sea in any way—"

"I know how!" one of the Monsters shouted.

She hated being interrupted by pathetic Monsters who dared to.

"Shut up, Lucas," another Monster whispered next to him and gave him a hard hit on the gut with his elbow.

"Thank you, Zach," Scarlet said to him. "Now, as I was saying, I need to see someone who can navigate in any way on the ocean. But, before you do that, you will all need training for whatever you find in the East, just in case. The Navigator can come with me. The rest of you get to work". She finished her instructions, and with the Monster who could navigate, she left the army. They headed to the Fortress and were guided by her trusted Royal Guards who had just caught up. She put on her game face as they headed to the Map Room.

Chapter 4

The beginning

I packed some supplies and I tried to think of what else I would need. This was what I packed:

A map.

A photo of our friends in case we miss them.

A water bottle.

Some food, and my Diamond Rapier, which I carry with me all the time.

I turned to Bucky and asked, "Almost done buddy?"

"Almost," he replied and packed one last thing into his backpack. "Done!"

Then my Amulet glowed on my Diamond chestplate; I got a message. I listened to the voice in my head. "Hey, Charles."

The voice of Atom said in my head, "Can you two come for a sec? I'm just outside of the ship," he asked us.

I replied while I listened. "Yeah, Atom, we're coming". Then we both went to find him. We did eventually, and followed him outside until we saw a boat that could fit me and Bucky in perfectly.

"I built it this morning because I thought of what Bucky said. He's right, I thought. You two will survive," he said to us, then looked down to Bucky, "You're smart," he said to him, impressed.

Bucky smiled at him.

I touched my Amulet and said, "We'll be leaving very soon, I promise we will survive. We'll be waiting at the shore for you all".

A moment later, everyone else arrived and we gave each other big hugs for good luck. After I hugged seven of them, I came to Chuckboi who had a frown on his face and I gave him a hug. He wrapped his arms and tail around me and whispered, "Be careful out there, Charlie."

"I will, Chuckboi," I said back to him, smiling.

Bucky and I boarded the boat, I grabbed the oars and I rowed for the journey.

"Good luck!" everyone shouted from the shore,

"Bye!" Bucky shouted back, waving and smiling on the boat. I saluted the others and continued rowing. Finally, we reached the ocean and turned East.

The journey had begun!

Chapter 5

The East

I rowed until home was a long way behind and I was exhausted from rowing. The sky was blue, the sun was out and it was burning hot! It was good that we brought our bottles so we wouldn't dehydrate or dry out.

"Don't you feel like having a drink, Bucky?" I asked him while I huffed and puffed from rowing.

He nodded. We took out our bottles from our backpacks to have a quick drink. That was when I realised I forgot to pack the Sun Sac! I smacked my forehead and groaned.

"What's wrong, Charlie?" Bucky asked.

"I'm such an idiot! I forgot the Sun Sac!" I replied.

"Relax, Charlie. I have it. We should put some on," Bucky said.

I sighed with relief. He grabbed his backpack from next to him and took out a small sac of sun gel. He passed the Sun Sac to me and I put some on my arms, legs and face. I passed it back to him and he put some on too; he rubbed his smooth cheeks then looked at me. "Oh *wow*, Charlie! That's a lot you put on!"

"You're thinking of my skin again".

"Oh right, Sorry," he said, chuckling nervously.

Sometimes he thinks that because my skin is bright.

Suddenly, we heard a deep roar in the water. Bucky was startled and rushed over to me and wrapped his tiny arms around my chestplate like a frightened child. I put one hand on him and the other on my weapon, just in case. We looked around the surface of the boat, the roar grew louder and louder until suddenly…

SPLASH!

A huge Long-Finned Leviathan jumped out of the water and flew over our boat. We screamed with horror as the Leviathan dived back into the sea, making another huge splash. Bucky let go of me and quickly rushed back to the other side of the boat. I didn't know why until I got saturated heavily, and he started giggling at me. I splashed him back with a bit of water for payback and giggled too. Then, we started splashing each other some more.

We splashed and splashed each other until there was a little bigger splash on the side of Bucky and he lifted his blue hand up quickly, I thought he almost got bitten by something in the water. He yelped in fear and he was breathing rapidly. His pupils shrunk to small dots and most of the teal iris filled his pupils, then he looked at me.

"Maybe we should stop," he said.

"We probably should," I agreed. "What do you want to do now?"

"I don't know, do you have any ideas?"

"Well… we could, um… watch the clouds."

"That sounds good to me."

Then we lay down and watched the passing clouds.

We watched the sky and chatted for an hour. "When that Long-Finned Leviathan jumped over our boat, I thought it would've been funny to watch you get wet," Bucky said.

"So that's why you ran to the other side of the boat, to let me get wet," I said back to him.

He snickered. "Yes."

"You're a nutbag," I said to him with a chuckle.

He threw back his head and laughed.

Then, I took in a big breath after chuckling softly, and let out a huge sigh. Bucky did the same eventually when he calmed down completely.

"I miss everyone already. Don't you, Charlie?" he asked me.

"All the time, when we're apart. I brought a photo with me. Here, I'll take it out". I went to my backpack and rummaged through it and took out the photo of all of us together. I passed it to Bucky and he stared at it for a little while. "Now that we are in the middle of nowhere in the East, and sailors have died here, I hope we won't end up like them too," he said worriedly.

"We won't buddy. I promise."

Suddenly, we heard an explosion from the distant horizon behind me.

"Did you hear that?" Bucky asked me. I turned around and looked ahead. My eyes widened with fear. "That's not good," I said.

"What?" he asked me. I pointed in front of me and Bucky looked.

"Oh no! That is *not* good!" He sounded terrified. We were heading into a storm! The storm started getting closer, and closer, and closer until it hit us.

"Hold on! We're gonna get us out of here!" I shouted to Bucky as he rushed to me and held on to me tight. I quickly grabbed the oars and began rowing as fast as I could. But the waves below us pulled us deeper in the storm.

"Hang on!" I shouted.

Bucky held my chestplate even tighter. The light of the sky was covered by the storm clouds and the waves were savage. The waves took us way up high and down again. It repeated until I got seasick and lost my grip on both oars. They floated on the surface until they were both swallowed up by the sea. We were in big trouble now and there was nothing we could do.

Eventually we were flipped over by a giant wave and it threw both of us off the boat and we fell into the sea. I looked around for Bucky in the water, and I found him struggling to swim because of the rough water. I swam to him, grabbed him and pushed up to the surface. We looked around for the boat, but it was gone. The waves towered above us and sucked us up and down in the water. Luckily, we still held onto each other tightly. Suddenly, a huge wave came after us. It rose higher and higher and then plunged towards us faster and closer until everything went black.

Chapter 6

A peek by the Sorcerer

Scarlet and her Monster kept planning on when they would find the two Alphas. Scarlet was really desperate, more than Charlie was.

"If you find the land they are on, place your boats on the sandbank high. You will also never know what's out there, you must stay together and battle ready for what comes in your way," she told the Monster who could navigate. "Take this compass." She took out a kind of compass from her black robe and showed it to him. It was no ordinary compass. "This will track down the two Alphanians,"

He claimed the compass and his eyes widened. "Thank you, your Highness."

"Your Highness, I need to show you something privately," a Sorcerer entered the room. He wore a dark purple robe that covered his toeless feet. His robe had a collar and sleeves braced by gold bands above his grey hands. There was a purple lining around his collar and on the front of his robe. His eyes were glowing dark-blue and his pupils and lens were glowing white like the other Monsters. He had a vertical scar on his left eye and had long thin brows with a gap in the left. Scarlet came to him and her Guards followed.

"Stay with the Navigator," she ordered them by looking at them by her shoulder.

"Yes, your Highness," they both said, respecting her orders, and kneeled before her with their deadly maces. Then she went with the Sorcerer.

A strong storm was building and it made everything darker outside. Scarlet followed the Sorcerer into the Dark Magic Chamber, straight to where the Sorcerer focused his mind on important things.

"What have you found, Jack?" she asked him using his real name.

"The Diamond Alpha and her little pal were caught in a storm," the Sorcerer explained. "But I found a nearby island where the two of them were swept upon."

"Are there any secrets on that island?" Scarlet asked.

"I don't know yet. But while I was looking around, this is what I found." The Sorcerer closed his eyes for two seconds, and stretched his arms out with his hands opened. Then he opened his eyes, this time they were glowing completely white. Then, while using magic, an image appeared in front of them.

Scarlet's scarred eye widened with satisfaction, "That's brilliant, Jack. Brilliant!" she shouted with sinister glee. The Sorcerer closed his bright eyes again and lowered his outstretched arms and the image disappeared. Then she started evil laughter and lightning struck outside as she laughed. When she calmed down and her laughter ceased, she said to herself, "Oh this is gonna be fun."

Then she smiled her evil smile again, showing her teeth.

Chapter 7

Deserted

I felt something cool and rough. There was bright light outside my eyes, I heard calm waves, squawking of wild birds and something nearby. I slowly woke up, sat up and shook my head because I was dizzy after that storm. I found myself on a beach with the ocean surrounding me. I was covered in sand too. I brushed the sand off my body and my pink hair. My hair felt a bit pointy on each end and that made me realise my hair was out.

I looked around the sand for my scrunchie, which I always wore; it wasn't anywhere to be seen. But luckily, I saw Bucky and he was alive, but he was choking!

I quickly got up and rushed over to him, wrapped him in both of my arms and squeezed his belly. I did dozens of tries until on the last one, I squeezed him even harder and finally, he coughed up a thing and it flew onto the sand. It was my scrunchie covered in saliva.

I stared at it with eyes wide. "Huh. Did not see that coming," I said unexpectedly.

I put Bucky down so he could catch his breath, he nearly collapsed. I walked up and grabbed my scrunchie. Then I walked to the water and soaked it to get rid of all his saliva.

I tied my hair back up again after soaking it for about ten seconds. I felt it was saturating my hair only a little bit, but I didn't mind at all. Then I walked to Bucky and helped him up.

"You alright, buddy?" I asked him.

He nodded as he shook the sand off his body and tail. Then he noticed something in the water behind me.

"My backpack!" he cried. He went straight to it.

I watched him as he grabbed it from the edge of the water. He opened it to check if everything was in there. The only thing he found was his small round water bottle. He took it out, opened the lid and tilted it to see if there was any drinking water in it.

None. Not even a drop. He lowered it down and looked at his feet. Then, I noticed his head turning red, like he was going to explode. He turned around to face me and shouted at me.

"*This…is all…your fault!*"

I froze in horror and watched him storm towards me.

"*We're stuck here because many of reasons: You wanted to go east! We lost the boat! We got caught in a storm! We almost lost everything and we are stuck on a stupid, deserted island with no supplies! There's nothing we can do! And if there's nothing we can do, we will have to live the rest.. of…our lives on this…deserted island.*"

Bucky looked all around and waved his arms like mad during his angry yelling, his volume decreased for some weird reason, and he slowed down. "I just saw something," he said, pointing to a jungle on the left of us.

I looked to where he pointed, and I saw nothing but the green and tropicalness in my sight. I stared at the jungle and very slowly my eyes grew larger with curiosity.

Bucky realised what I was thinking, and hid behind my back with a nervous look. "Are you…are you going to explore this unknown jungle?" he asked me nervously.

I stood up and he hid behind my legs. "Well, you can say that," I replied.

He put his backpack on and we started walking towards the jungle, feeling nervous. Before I took a step on the soil, I heard a sigh of relief from Bucky.

"What?" I asked him.

"You still have your weapon," he answered. I placed my hand on my back and felt something cool and smooth: my Diamond Rapier. I was glad I still had it, just in case we were ambushed by anything that lurked inside the jungle.

As we took our first steps on the soil in the jungle and deeper away from the shore, we saw lots and lots of flora. As we ventured, we first encountered a flock of lorikeets that had black feathers that looked like mandibles on their heads and their bodies were orange as a mandarin. They flew towards us and one landed on Bucky's head. He was frightened by them, so I shooed the birds away from him, and they all flew away, squawking loudly.

We kept on exploring and found a few blooming shrubs and they were very, very beautiful. The first one we found had white flowers that looked like they wore a dress and their wings were made from their own beautiful petals. We had some of those shrubs on the mainland too in the Oceanic Mountainside; the Singanoids called them Ballerina Flowers. They can be used for decorating and they are edible as well. Then, Bucky found another shrub nearby and went to investigate. That one he found was pretty; It had blending colours of green and blue.

The flowers were shut though, but when Bucky was about to take a closer look, it spat an oozing liquid on his blue nose. I laughed until I was spat by one too and then we both laughed. We laughed and laughed until suddenly, we heard a noise in the bushes.

I took out my weapon and Bucky ran to me, startled. I brushed the ooze off my face and quickly looked around for any danger. Then I saw a bush shaking. I moved closer to the bush with my weapon pointing at it. The shaking grew and more dramatic until suddenly, a creature popped out of it, but it was just a Dragonfly. I had a fright when it popped out, but I thought it was just a false alarm.

I heard Bucky rapidly breathing. I turned to him who hid behind me. "It's alright buddy, it's just a false alarm," I said.

"I saw it right over there!" he shouted, nearly hyperventilating. Bucky pointed to a small dark area with his tiny blue hand. I looked, but I couldn't see anything.

I looked at him again and kneeled in front of him. "Relax, Bucky," I said, "I'm sure it's fine. Here, hold my hand or crawl into my backpack if you need to."

Bucky wanted to hold my hand, so I held out my hand to him; he grabbed it with his hand and we moved on.

'

Chapter 8

The first wild night

It got dark eventually and we hadn't found shelter yet. We kept searching. Bucky said to me before night came that his feet hurt from walking for most of the afternoon and he was tired, so I had to carry him. He was asleep now.

I was cold in the breeze, so was Bucky; I felt him shivering in my arms. I didn't want him to be cold all night, so I looked around to find anything that would be useful. I found a few large green leaves that must have fallen off tall trees. I leaned down and picked one up with one hand and held Bucky in the other. The leaf I picked up was just about the right size for him. I laid it on him and he stopped shivering; he must have felt warmer. I kept walking in the darkness with him sleeping protected in my warm arms.

I was really tired now and like Bucky's feet from earlier, mine were sore too. I felt like I was going to collapse, but I kept pushing through the jungle.

Finally, we found shelter. It was a small area protected from the cold breeze surrounded by bushes and long vines, also leaving enough space inside. I walked into it, moving the vines out of the way and gently laid Bucky down with the leaf still on him, and then I went to find sticks.

As I was outside, I didn't want to waste much time collecting too many sticks. So I grabbed like ten sticks and thought that would do. I decided to turn back and along the way, I found a large stick thickness of like three sticks merged together. I grabbed that stick and continued on.

I returned to the shelter eventually, and Bucky was in a deep sleep. I put all the sticks down and shaped the smaller ones into a small teepee. Then I grabbed the larger stick and spun on top of it as fast as I could. I made a couple of sparks, and then the sticks began smoking. I blew them carefully until they lit to fire successfully. It lit up the inside of the vines that shielded us from the wind. The fire was also warming the area very quickly and I was warm as though I was in my own blanket.

I rubbed my eyes, laid down next to Bucky and smiled at him as he slept peacefully, and then I rested mine. I thought it was such a big day after being swept up on an island in the middle of nowhere in the East, and we had finally found somewhere to rest.

Chapter 9

An unexpected mystery

Scarlet and the Monster finished their first plan and Scarlet sent one group that had two Monsters, five Monster Archers and the Navigator to the shore. They boarded their boats and set off East. The Sorcerer stayed outside and watched them row away from the land. When they were far enough, he closed his eyes to watch the group in his mind.

The group rowed away from the bank and reached the ocean, they rowed for a long time. The Navigator led the way using the compass Scarlet gave him.

He turned to the group and said, "We need to keep moving and find the Alphanians. We cannot afford to lose!"

But one groaned in exhaustion and asked idiotically, "Can't we just take one now, Lucas? We've been rowing from the mainland to here without any sleep."

"We can't, Samuel, and that's a stupid idea, because three words: Hybrainian-eating creatures," the Navigator answered.

"**He's right, Sam. We need to keep moving, otherwise we're fish bait**," a Monster Archer said in another boat next to him. The tired Monster growled in frustration.

"**Hey look over there! There's an island!**" another Monster Archer shouted, pointing to an island in front of them. The Navigator looked at the compass, the arrow pointed to the island in front of them.

"That must be where they are. Head to the island!" he commanded the others, and they rowed to the island.

They reached the beach and pulled their boats up high enough so they wouldn't drift away. They grabbed their weapons and supplies and entered the jungle. They were nervous and prepared. They heard the breeze, the bushes and trees waving smoothly. They kept their eyes and ears peeled for any danger that may lurk there.

They stayed cautious as they moved in the darkness together until suddenly, they heard a quick muffled grunt that came from one of them, who then mysteriously disappeared. They stopped and looked around until they heard another Monster Archer grunt and disappear unseen. There were only six of them left now: one Monster Minion, four Monster Archers and the Navigator.

They came closer together, and five of them raised their weapons. Suddenly they heard a sound of a whizzing stab on the Monster Minion's arm, and he fell to the ground. Now there were five of them left. Each of them was facing a different direction. The Navigator panicked after the four Monster Archers dropped like flies. He sweated and shivered with fear. He was alone now. His heart raced almost faster than a mouse's. "Leave me alone!" he shouted, panicking.

Too frightened to move, the Navigator froze. Then two glowing brown eyes appeared behind the Navigator with a weapon. Slowly and silently, the weapon rose above the Navigator's head, swung up high and hit him hard on the side. The Navigator fell unconscious on the ground with the others.

Back at the Fortress the Sorcerer was losing focus on the group in his mind. He opened his eyes quickly with shock after something took down the group. His breathing was unsteady with fear. He turned around and faced the Fortress that towered in front of him. He needed to report to the Fire Queen about what happened. He started running for the Fortress.

Chapter 10

The Survival

Bucky and I managed to survive the night and we continued exploring the jungle. Unfortunately, our stomachs growled a lot and Bucky was thirsty. We searched for food and water. We searched for hours until I found something that made me stop and stare desperately.

Bucky bumped into my legs without paying attention to what was in front of him.

"Charlie?" he said. He walked in front of me, went up onto his toes and waved his hand in front of my face. He whistled, "Charlie? Hello?" He went down from his tippy toes, then looked at what I was staring at. His eyes widened.

"A river!" we both shouted. We dashed to the river to drink. As we drank, some water went down the wrong way while I drank, and I coughed.

"Are you alright?" he asked me.

"Water went down the wrong way" I replied while I coughed.

Bucky took out his bottle from his backpack and filled it with the running water. I took mine out too and did the same.

After our drink from the river, we searched for food. I was hungry and Bucky was starving—I would survive forever, technically, but Bucky wouldn't. Then, we found a bush that had hundreds of rainberries. Rainberries got their name because of all the colourful berries growing on them. We came up to the bush and picked out the good ones and ate them. Now after a drink from the river and our bellies full of rainberries, we explored without needing anything more.

Bucky was a little behind me.

I turned to him and said, "I need to say, Bucky, this island is rich! Atom would love to hear this when we find a way home".

"Yeah, he will," Bucky said, agreeing but sceptical when I said 'find a way home', but he'd get over it.

We explored over an hour, and discovered lots of things like Spidopillars, Dragonflies, Green Shroomlings and much more. Then we found colourful bushes

I was amazed by all the colours. I went up to them and picked out a blue one, a green one and an orange one from a single bush. I then put them together and said to myself, "Multicoloured shrubs?"

But before I stored the samples for Atom to study, I heard Bucky scream. I got a fright. I turned around and saw him moving unsteadily, then he fell to the ground grunting heavily in pain.

"Bucky!" I cried. I ran to him and tried to help him up, but he felt heavy and pale. Shockingly, I noticed an object on his arm: a dart!

We were ambushed!

I quickly pulled out my Diamond Rapier and shot out my battle look. "Whoever or whatever you are, show yourself!" I shouted into the trees and coloured shrubs. I heard rattling in the bushes surrounding us and I saw two glowing brown eyes. Then a figure shot out from the darkness, grabbed a vine, swung to a tree and slid down to the ground in front of us, showing a spear. My eyes widened in fascination. It was a red male Singanoid! But he looked very different.

He wore pants made from large leaves, a brown side belt with a striped patterned neck wrap. Colourful bracelets were on each wrist. His face was painted; blue lines on top of his forehead, and lime survival markings on his cheeks. There was an aquatic-like pattern between his eyes and the pattern of flame on the top of his dotted nose. Unlike Tar and Stephenie with colourful hair, he was bald.

I thought the island was deserted, I thought. Then I refocused on the Singanoid. I pointed my weapon at him, ready for a fight. He moved slowly towards us with his weapon pointing. Then he began to move faster and faster, then jumped high up and pointed his spear at Bucky. I blocked him just in time, and we fought each other. The

Singanoid was pretty strong, but he wasn't stronger than me. I tried to get him with my weapon, but he dodged it and tried to hit me. I blocked it and pushed him hard away from us.

I had enough time to look back. Bucky was on the ground with the dart on his arm, looking very weak. I watched him as he slowly closed his eyes, then he collapsed to the ground, his eyes still closed. My heart raced after that shocking moment and my eyes widened with fear.

Eventually I looked back at the Singanoid coming towards us, and I was boiling with fury.

"Oh! You are going to pay for this!" I shouted. I blinked and my eyes glowed sky blue, my iris was purply pink and my pupils were black. I brought up my fist and spun it faster and faster as the Singanoid quickly came closer. Then he jumped into the air and tried to whack me with his spear. I gave him a powerful blow on his gut and he flew above the ground and hit a tree behind him. He hit the ground and put one hand on his stomach and grunted heavily in pain, and it showed a tattoo… of my Mindatar symbols!

I was terrified when I saw it. I blinked again and my eyes were back to normal. I looked at the Singanoid miserably and he stared at me with his brown eyes. I slowly backed away, then I grabbed Bucky and ran deeper into the jungle.

Chapter 11

The Singanoid's truth

I was terribly shocked by the tattoo the Singanoid had. I ran and I carried Bucky deeper and deeper in the jungle until it was night-time. I didn't know where we were going, and realised we were lost. I thought if we stayed out in the darkness for too long, the Singanoid would find us and try to kill Bucky. I didn't want that to happen. I passed many trees and bushes as I walked with Bucky, who lay motionless in my arms.

Eventually after walking a while in the darkness, I found another area nearby. It was a dirt wall with lots of space on the brown ground and fireflies on the side of a bush beside the wall. But sadly, it was dark and cold there, but I had no choice, we needed somewhere to hide and rest. So I went there to put Bucky down and went looking for sticks as soon as possible.

Nearby I found a few bushes that did the trick. I rummaged into them and grabbed a handful of thin sticks and one that was thicker. I returned to Bucky after that and made a small teepee in the middle. Then I spun the largest stick until they started smoking, and blew them until they lit to fire. I felt warm again, but very miserable. I crawled to Bucky, lying on the ground as though he was in deep sleep, and sat on my knees in front of him. I smacked him gently in the face a few times saying, "C'mon, Bucky. Wake up".

I tried and tried faithfully, but sadly nothing worked. I opened one of his eyes, but it closed after I let go. My eyes flooded with tears and they slithered on my cheeks, and my gut filled with butterflies.

I picked Bucky up and laid his head on my shoulder and I said in a trembling voice, "Oh, Bucky, what should I do? What should I do? What have I done to get you into this? You were right all along, this is all my fault."

Another tear slithered on my cheek, and dropped onto Bucky's blue nose. I knew he'd been right all along; it was my fault that we ended up on the island.

Suddenly, I noticed a shadow. I turned and looked. It was the Singanoid with a worried look on his face.

I gave him a glare and said, "Go away!" but he didn't move. He came closer to us, I pushed his chest, "Back off!" I snapped at him.

He stood on his feet again, but he didn't leave.

I stared at him in annoyance and shouted "Leave us *alone!*"

He flinched only a little bit.

"What do you want from us?!" I shouted at him, almost crying with anger, he didn't say anything. Then, he leaned his spear on the dirt wall, and put one hand to his back, probably to grab something.

I pulled Bucky closer to me just to protect him until unexpectedly, the Singanoid pulled out a

63

glowing blue object. My eyes widened and I recognised what he had in his hand: it was lemunity.

He slowly reached out the other hand to Bucky and the tip of his red fingers gently touched his cheek, and then he looked at me. I was unsure if I could trust him.

"Can I trust you?" I asked him with a sad snuffle.

He nodded.

"A hundred percent?"

He nodded again.

I gave Bucky a gentle squeeze and another tear slithered down my cheek, and then I passed him to the Singanoid. He laid him on his lap and lifted up Bucky's arm where he'd shot his dart, and carefully took it out. Bucky's arm bled after he did. The Singanoid looked at me, then pointed to a bush. I understood what he wanted; he wanted a leaf.

Before I went, I asked him, "You're not much of a talker, are you?"

He didn't answer or move his head. Then I got up and went to the bush he pointed at, and grabbed a small, long thin leaf. I went back to the Singanoid and gave him what he needed. He wrapped it around Bucky's arm like a bandage.

"Wow. You know survival very well," I admitted, and the Singanoid chuckled. He put one hand on the leaf on Bucky's arm to stop it from unwrapping and looked around to find something to prevent it.

I had an idea. I took out my hair and showed the scrunchie to the Singanoid. He saw it and looked at me, and realised what I was trying to do. He grabbed my scrunchie, and tied it on the leafy bandage. We finally completed it.

Next, the Singanoid picked up the Iemunity, took off the lid and used his other hand to open Bucky's mouth, and accidentally poked one crimson finger on Bucky's left bottom fang and he shook his hand in the air. Eventually he carefully tilted the lemunity and poured one quarter of it in Bucky's mouth. Then he closed his mouth and rubbed Bucky's tiny neck until he felt him swallow it. Then he passed him back to me.

I had a smile on my face and said gracefully, "Thank you."

He smiled back.

But then, my smile went upside down and I asked him, "But when is he going to wake up?"

His smile faded and he didn't answer and looked down.

"It's okay, I understand," I said, looking to the ground, feeling hopeless, and more tears ran down my cheeks. "We should…um… better leave you alone." I got up and walked towards the darkness with Bucky.

Before we vanished in the darkness, there was a response. "Don't Charlie, it's alright to stay here," the Singanoid finally spoke.

I turned to him, surprised. "How do you know my name?" I asked him.

"I'm Hajuan. We are true believers of you. We were hoping you would come," he answered.

I was more surprised. *A Tribe of Singanoids from another place believed in me and hoped that I would come? I never knew that before,* I thought. "Well, Hajuan, it's nice to meet you." I came back and shook his hand, then I put Bucky down to rest on the wall of dirt. Then I remembered what happened and I asked Hajuan, "I apologise for attacking you. But, why did you attack him?"

"I thought he was attacking you, I was just trying to protect you," Hajuan answered.

"But he's my friend," I said.

Hajuan sighed. "I found a group of trespassers last night. They had strange weapons. I haunted them myself, and then took them out unseen. I tossed them in their boats and pushed them out into the sea, ready to be annihilated. When you and your friend arrived, I was there, watching you both. Your friend saw me and before he was going to show you, I ran straight back to my village to tell the Tribe. The

67

chiefs sent me out with a ceremony of faith that night, and before I left, my special girl came to me. I pulled her to me, while I held my spear," he explained, looking heartwarmed.

"What's your girl's name?" I asked him with a smile.

"Ching Ching. I'm in love with her. When me and Ching Ching have our ceremony, we'll be the next chiefs."

I nodded while looking at the ground, then I asked him another question. "Hajuan, when you said 'ready to be annihilated', what do you mean about that?"

"I throw trespassers into the sea, and the Long-Finned Leviathans will wipe them out. But they will never do that to you and your Alphas, especially your little pal," he answered truthfully.

"Oh. Before we came to your island, we heard a large roar under our boat. We both looked at the surface to see what was going on, until a Long-Finned Leviathan jumped over our boat. Bucky and I screamed as it dived back into the sea.

Bucky let go of me, and ran to the other side and I got wet," I told Hajuan with a giggle, he imagined it was funny too.

"They were probably happy to see you," Hajuan said.

"Really? How do you know?"

"They do look blind, but it's the opposite," he answered.

"Oh, Okay," I said, understanding and surprised. Then I looked at his spear still leaning on the dirt wall and asked, "You're a warrior, aren't you?"

"The strongest and stealthiest warrior in my village. This is why I'm here," he answered and looked at me and asked, "Why?"

"I was just curious," I said. Then I noticed the tattoo on his hand. It gave me the memory of when I first saw it, but I didn't know what it meant. So I asked him, "That tattoo of my symbols. Is there a purpose for it?"

"The tattoo of your symbols is there to show how much you inspire us with your imagination.

We knew the old legend of when you were born as a Youth, as you grew, you became you. And we also knew one time in the future, you will come to our land and we'd greet you with a ceremony when it's a full Silver Moon only two days away. Now that you're finally here, I can take you both to my village tomorrow," he said.

"I think your people will love that," I said.

"Oh, they will," Hajuan replied, agreeing with a smile.

I yawned and rubbed my eyes. "Well, we should get some rest," I said to Hajuan.

He agreed and laid down with a stretch. "Goodnight, Charlie."

"Goodnight, Hajuan," I said back. I watched him as he put his hands under his head and closed his eyes, his chest rising and falling. I turned to Bucky next to me and said quietly, "Goodnight, Bucky". I hoped he would wake up the next day. Then I touched my sapphire Amulet and said to our friends back home, "Goodnight, everyone. We miss you, and we're okay." Then I laid down and rested my eyes. I honestly didn't really expect to meet another Singanoid in the middle of the East, hoping that I would come for a sacred ceremony, I assumed.

Chapter 12

Scarlet's ultimate weapon

"Bad news, your highness! I lost the group in my mind," the Sorcerer shouted as he hurriedly ran to Scarlet.

She turned around and shouted alarmed, "What? How!"

"I don't know," he replied.

"What do you mean 'you don't know'?" she questioned him. She hovered on top of the Sorcerer with an angry look on her face, and the Sorcerer fell to the ground.

"I…I don't know," he said to her with a worried look.

"*Just* tell me! *What* did you see?! Give me detail, you idiot!" Scarlet yelled, her hair blowing into larger flames. The Sorcerer was worried she would end up in another Wild Rage. In a Wild Rage, Scarlet will scream dramatically and her body will completely blow into flames and make a fire explosion.

"The group disappeared from something," he said to her.

"'From something'?" she questioned again, not really surprised.

"Yes," the Sorcerer said.

Scarlet scoffed, then turned and hovered away to give the Sorcerer some space to get up. She faced her throne and her body shook with anger. "I've had *enough* of this! But it's not over yet. Time for Plan B!" she said to herself. Looking over to the Sorcerer again, she demanded, "We need to see the Captain, I'll need *you* to explain."

They left the Throne Room and passed the chambers of the Fortress to the Training Ground outside. The other Monsters saw them and kneeled down to them as they headed to the captain.

The Captain saw them. "**What do you need, your Highness?**"

"We need to speak with you," she replied to him.

"**Anything, your Majesty**," he said.

73

"Well..." the Sorcerer began. "I discovered in my mind that something, with a tattoo of the symbols of the Mindatar, neutralized the group. I'm not sure what it is yet, but we need a plan," he explained to the captain.

"Hmm." the captain said. "What is your plan, your Highness?"

"Forget the darn planning, I got one already. Captain, send... the R.A.I.D!"

(Rampaging Army of Indestructible Doom).

Chapter 13

Bucky

I saw the light from inside my eyes, I heard the birds chirping and my breathing, and I felt two things on my hip.

"Charlie?" a familiar voice said.

I slowly sat up and rubbed my eyes.

"Hi, Charlie," the voice said.

I slowly woke up, then looked to my left and gasped in excitement, "Bucky!" I wrapped him in my arms and pulled him to me, "You're awake! I knew that you'll wake up," I said to him gleefully.

He lay his head on my shoulder, "I'm awake now, Charlie. But, what happened?"

"I knocked you out with one of my darts," Hajuan said nearby. Bucky looked over his shoulder and his eyes widened. I let go of him so he could see Hajuan a little closer.

"I saw you when we washed up here," Bucky said, fascinated.

Hajuan kneeled to Bucky's level.

"Bucky, this is Hajuan," I said.

Hajuan gave out his hand to give Bucky a handshake, but Bucky was shy, and stayed close to me.

"It's okay buddy. He won't hurt us again, I promise," I said, hoping to see if that would help him.

He asked me, "Are you sure?"

"I'm one hundred percent sure buddy".

"O…okay," he said. He slowly walked away from me and straight to Hajuan. He nervously reached out his blue tiny shaking hand towards Hajuan's. Hajuan grabbed his hand and gently shook it.

Bucky pulled his hand away after they finished, and smiled at him.

"He's very short," Hajuan commented.

Bucky's smile faded and he glared at him. Bucky doesn't like being called short.

"Um, Hajuan, he doesn't like being called 'short'," I reminded him.

76

"Oh, Sorry. I take back what I said," Bucky smiled again and accepted his apology. Hajuan got up and Bucky came back to me, "So, are you two ready yet?" he asked us.

"'Ready'? For what?" Bucky asked, puzzled.

"Hajuan's going to take us to his village," I answered, and then replied to Hajuan, "Yes, we're ready".

"Good. We should get a move on then," Hajuan said.

"How far is your village from here?" I asked him.

"My village would be about a day's journey. But don't fret. I know the island by heart," he answered.

"Okay," I replied.

Chapter 14

Marandikeets

We were back in the jungle, but this time, accompanied by Hajuan. I was actually excited and wondered what his village would look like. I even thought about the Singanoids there and what they looked like, but soon, Bucky and I would learn more.

"How long have you lived here?" Bucky asked him.

"Ever since the beginning of my life," Hajuan answered.

Suddenly, we noticed shadows from a flock of familiar birds coming out of nowhere and flying above us. They were the same birds that we found after we were washed up on the island. They flew towards us, Bucky got frightened and hid behind me. Most of the birds flew towards the two of us and one flew right in front of me. The others flew playfully around Bucky and I and made me giggle.

I extended out my arm so they could land on it, one did.

"Aawww," I said, awed by the beautiful creature. I turned to Bucky. "It's okay buddy. I have one on my arm, give it a pat, it won't bite you," I said to him.

He looked up at me, still frightened, "No thank you," he said.

I smiled at him. "Okay, Bucky." I looked at the bird on my arm again with a smile, then to Hajuan. Hajuan had three of them on his arm. "What do you call these things?" I asked him with a satisfied chuckle.

"Whatever you call them," he replied.

I was confused. "Me?" I asked.

"It's a Mindatar's job to name everything, and we know you are creative," he answered.

"Oh, um...okay. I'll think about what I shall call them." I tried to think of what to call them. I looked at the black feathers on its face and the orange feathers on its body. I took it all in, and thought as hard as I could. "Marandikeets!" I shouted.

Hajuan and Bucky looked at me,

"Marandikeets?" Hajuan said.

"Yeah. Because the six black feathers on its face look like mandibles, and their feathers on their bodies are orange like a mandarin," I explained.

"That actually fits," Bucky said.

"That makes sense," Hajuan agreed, impressed with the name I gave the birds. I was proud of myself, it fitted perfectly. The Marandikeet on my arm started flapping its wings, then flew off my arm and up to the sky. The other Marandikeets followed and they all flew away, we watched them.

Bucky emerged from behind my legs.

"That was incredible," I said.

"I'm glad you liked it," Hajuan said with a smile.

Since we first met Hajuan one night ago, he'd been awesome! If it wasn't for him, Bucky would never have woken up and we would be in big trouble. We were so lucky to have him as a friend.

Chapter 15

The surprise

We kept following Hajuan. I had to carry Bucky for the past ten minutes because his feet were hurting again and he was really tired. I was tired from walking for most of the day too.

Hajuan never gave up though until he heard our stomachs growling. "Hungry?" he asked us.

I nodded.

"Don't worry, I have some food".

"We should sit down and eat," I said.

"Alright," he said.

We found a place nearby for the night and Hajuan took out a coconut filled with red prawns. He opened it and placed the jar in the middle. I woke Bucky up and let him know we were going to eat. We each took out a red prawn and Hajuan ate it, but I didn't.

I just stared at it curiously and asked Hajuan, "What are these?"

"They're Fireshrimp, they're very nutritious, but they're spicy when they're cooked. One of my favourites," he answered, taking out a second prawn.

Bucky didn't take any because Gippyguppies are omnivores; they do also eat tiny aquatic creatures like shrimps. But he was more vegetarian. Hajuan could see he was really hungry, so he passed his second one to him.

Bucky looked at it and looked at him, "Uhh…no thanks, Hajuan. I don't eat meat."

But instead of Hajuan taking it and eating it, he kindly insisted, "You do sound very hungry, I insist even when you don't eat meat".

Bucky's growling stomach agreed, He thought it was true if he took it. So he did, "Thanks, Hajuan." He placed the Fireshrimp in his mouth to taste it. "This is actually not bad. This isn't spicy," he said while munching. Then after a few seconds, Bucky's mouth turned red and he started breathing rapidly. He took out his bottle from his backpack and drank. "I must've spoken too soon," he said after a gulp of water.

I cackled and Hajuan chuckled.

"I was once like that, but I got used to them," Hajuan replied.

"Really?" I asked him, he nodded.

He saw my Fireshrimp still in my hand. "Give it a try, Charlie. They're really good," he said.

I shrugged and tossed the Fireshrimp into my mouth. It was a little spicy, but it was really good. "These are really good. Where do you find these things?" I asked Hajuan.

"They come up to the surface every Summer to breed," he answered.

It slowly started getting dark. I thought of making another fire to keep us warm and safe. "I should gather some sticks for fire, I'll be right back," I said.

"Charlie, wait, before you go, I want to tell you both something."

"What is it?" Bucky and I both asked him at the same time. "I want to show you something high up in the trees tonight, it's a surprise," he said.

I loved surprises.

We watched the sky as it got darker and my eyes began glowing and I wondered what the surprise was. I pictured swirling bright nebulas in the night sky, or fireflies glowing above like stars, but whatever the surprise was, I hope it was breathtaking.

"It's time. Follow me," Hajuan said to us, getting up.

I turned to him, and noticed his eyes unexpectedly glowing.

"Whoa!" I shouted.

"What?" Hajuan said, looking at me.

"Your eyes are glowing!"

"Oh, that. I've been hunting in the darkness for years, my eyes became used to it. Your eyes are glowing too," Hajuan said.

"Oooohh, right, yeah. You have a point," I said, "That's a new one."

"C'mon," Hajuan said. He came up to a tree and started climbing. Bucky climbed onto my back and I began climbing too. Hajuan wasn't too far above us and we were far from the ground now. I didn't want to look down because I'd hyperventilate. As we got closer to the top, Hajuan was up there, waiting for us.

I asked Bucky, "Can you get up there buddy?"

"I'll try," he replied. He climbed off my back and on top of my head and reached out for Hajuan, Hajuan grabbed his hand and lifted him up. Hajuan helped me up when I was almost there. I eventually reached the top.

I looked around for the surprise, all I saw were the leaves below us and the night sky above. "What's the surprise?" I asked Hajuan.

"Watch the largest tree," he replied.

We watched the largest trees in front of us, nothing was happening.

"Is... anything supposed to happen?"

"Wait for it," he said with a smile as he watched the tree. I narrowed my eyes to get a

86

better look, so did Bucky, and all of a sudden, the tree was sparkling! I was amazed with that discovery and so was Bucky.

"That's cool!" He shouted gleefully.

"That's amazing!" I said with satisfaction.

"We do it as a generation every year, watching the Droplet Tree," Hajuan said.

"Droplet Tree?" I asked.

"We called it the Droplet Tree because it collects the water from the ground to moist itself. It does it only once every year," he explained.

"You're so cool," I said, looking at Hajuan,

Bucky agreed.

Hajuan chuckled. "I accept that very much, thank you," he said, smiling.

I looked at the Droplet Tree, and sighed with enjoyment. "That is so beautiful," I said.

"It is, isn't it?" Hajuan said.

Bucky and I nodded.

Chapter 16

Sorcerer's revenge

They sent the R.A.I.D to find the two irritating Alphanians, Scarlet was sick of it. The other Monsters were in the buffet having Grumm—a Monster beer. Scarlet was on the veranda with her two trusted Royal Guards, who were drinking too, and she was looking to the ground with a frustrated look.

The Sorcerer appeared on the veranda, Scarlet knew he was there and sighed, "What do you want, Jack?"

"Nothing, your Highness," he answered. "Then why are you here?"

"I'm just here to check on you," he answered.

"I'm fine, Jack, thanks," she said.

"You are welcome, your Highness," he replied with a smile.

"Jack, I need to tell you something," she said, turning her head and looking back.

"Anything, your Highness," he said.

Scarlet walked to him and said, "I need you to fully inspect the R.A.I.D, and make sure everything is in progress. But there is one thing that is very important: make sure, the R.A.I.D succeeds,"

"And if it doesn't?" he asked her, feeling nervous. She reached out a hand without looking at her trusted Royal Guards and one of them passed their empty glasses to her and continued.

"Let's just say this glass is you, if I have discovered the R.A.I.D failed." She crushed the glass in her hand and the shards fell on the ground. Her Royal Guards and the Sorcerer were shocked when they saw that. One of her Royal Guards choked on his Grumm sending it down the wrong way, and he started hitting his chest. The Sorcerer nervously gulped and sweated with fear. He was worried about what would happen to him if she did discover the R.A.I.D failed.

"Promise me: the R.A.I.D will succeed," she said to the Sorcerer.

The Sorcerer cleared his throat and said, "I promise, your Majesty".

"He is *so* dead, if she finds out," one of her trusted Royal Guards whispered.

Scarlet clearly heard what he said and shouted angrily, "Shut up! I'm not in the mood right now! Jeez.

She left the veranda and headed inside the Fortress. "Well done, Frank," the other said, unimpressed, "What? Seriously, what did I do?" the one who whispered argued. They kept arguing.

The Sorcerer walked to the veranda and let out a huge sigh. "This is not good with the Diamond Alpha immortal, she will kill me."

"Well, Jack, you never know the chances if she does or not," one of the Royal Guards said.

"You're wrong, Phil, the Queen will kill me unless I think of something," the Sorcerer said.

"Well then, think of something, anything," the other said.

The Sorcerer tried to think. The Royal Guards continued arguing with each other, "It's not my fault for what happened! I, for Hybrainian's sake, just whispered to you!"

"You made the Queen stressed!"

"So!"

"It's not like a Monster with magic can defeat the Alpha!" they argued.

The Sorcerer's eyes quickly widened when he heard 'Monster with magic'. That gave him an idea.

"You know what?" he said.

"What!" They both shouted.

"I'm joining the R.A.I.D.," he replied with a look.

"What?" one asked, confused.

"But the R.A.I.D has already left," the other said.

"I'm a Sorcerer, I can summon Demons that can take me there," he replied.

"But, Jack, you're supposed to inspect the R.A.I.D.".

"That's a job for someone else now. I'm going to join the R.A.I.D.".

The two Royal Guards looked at each other. "We only send Monster Archers. Why are you doing this?"

"I am the Queen's only trusted Sorcerer. Now, things are going to change for me," he said, and left the veranda.

The two Royal Guards looked at each other again, unsure if it was a good idea, because that was actually against their Queen's rules, or even worse, you would get corrupted by the storm!

Chapter 17

Hajuan's Village

The night when Hajuan showed us the Droplet tree was just incredible, and now we were almost to his village. My excitement grew more and more as we, I believe, got closer. The space around us was much bigger than it was before and I noticed a few pointed things in front of us. As we got closer to them, Bucky and I realised, they aren't just things, it's a village with round teepees made from straw, except the wooden stage in front of us.

We must be here!

"*Ima ack! Ut Ima ot lone his ime!* (I'm back! But I'm not alone this time!)" Hajuan shouted to the village in the Hybrainian language. The Hybrainian language is a little confusing at first, but it's like taking the first letter in a word unless it's only by itself. It would be pronounced differently. We listened for a response, then

93

something emerged from the village tipis, a young male Singanoid.

"Hajuan's back!" The boy shouted.

Then, more Singanoids emerged from their homes and were excited to see us.

"Welcome to the Village of Cocoa," Hajuan said to us. The Tribe gathered and surrounded us, Bucky hid behind me, looking shy. Then, someone appeared from inside the Tribe in front of us, a small female blue Singanoid.

"Hajuan!" she shouted with glee, and ran to Hajuan and hugged him. The woman was very beautiful with blonde hair and a small bushy ponytail. She wore a traditional patterned half shirt and a skirt made from thread. There were freckles on her face. She even had a picture of my Mindatar symbols on her cheek. I noticed others in the Tribe have them too.

Hajuan's right, I thought, they are true believers.

"I'm so happy you came back," she said to Hajuan.

94

"I always will, my love," he said back to her with a heart-warmed smile and gave her a kiss on the cheek. Then, she saw me with her aqua-blue eyes widened with excitement.

"You're finally here!" she shouted.

Hajuan let go of her and she came towards me with a big smile. "After all these years, you finally came!" she said, and she and the others kneeled down on the ground, including Hajuan with his spear.

I was buzzing with amazement from the Singanoids words. I never knew more of them out there believed in me, but the truth was: I didn't know why.

"Now that you're here, we can do the ceremony when it's a full moon," she said, looking up at me.

"What's the ceremony?" I asked her.

"We can't tell you yet, Diamond Alpha," another Singanoid answered.

"Fair enough," I replied.

"My name is Ching Ching," the female Singanoid in front of me said.

"Hajuan has been telling me about you the night before," I replied. Ching Ching looked at Hajuan with a smile.

Hajuan's cheeks went blue. Depending on the Singanoid's coloured skin, their blood is different coloured too, in fact.

Bucky hid and peeked around the side of my legs a little bit with a curious look.

Ching Ching looked back to me and suddenly saw him, and Bucky hid behind my legs again. Ching Ching got up and walked behind me to get a closer look at him, but Bucky was shy. She stared at him as though she had never seen him before, she looked up and asked me.

"What is he?"

"He's a Gippyguppy," I said. "What's your Tribe?

"We are the Coconians," she said.

Then, some of the youngsters came and curiously stared at Bucky. They poked him, smelled him and grabbed his arms.

"Alright, alright, kids. Give him some space," I said while smiling at the children.

"Sorry, Diamond Alpha. We're just very curious," one of them said while they headed back to their families.

"It's alright," I said to them.

"It's all good," Bucky said.

Ching Ching looked at him.

"This is Bucky," I said, Bucky nodded.

"Oh, it's also very nice to meet you, little Gippyguppy," she said, and Bucky smiled.

"Before we show them the secret, we should show them around our village," Hajuan said to Ching Ching.

"I think that's a good idea," she agreed.

The Tribe thought it was too, so they got up and cleared a path in front of us.

Hajuan said to us with a smile "Follow me, I'll show you around."

Chapter 18

The studio

I was really excited to explore Hajuan's village and learn everything about it for the first time. The first things Bucky and I discovered in the village were the straw teepees, but there were more things I wanted to learn about. I wanted to learn how they lived, gathered, hunted and thrived. But soon, we'd learn more. We headed to a wooden building in front of us.

"This is the studio. It's where we get the painted tattoos of your Mindatar symbols and our faces marked. We usually get your symbols when we're about ten or higher," Hajuan explained.

"When did you get yours?" I asked him.

"I got mine when I was twelve," he replied.

"Can I get one?" Bucky asked.

"Knock yourself out kid," Hajuan said with a smile.

Bucky smiled and grabbed my hand and dragged me to an empty patterned mat in the studio with a face painter waiting.

The face painter told him to sit down and close his eyes, and he did just that. The face painter dipped two fingers into a small pot of ink and began drawing on Bucky's face. The face painter drew two yellow lines down from his forehead and to his cheeks. The tattoo maker then drew two blue survival marks on his cheeks and added my Mindatar symbols on his forehead. It honestly, to me, felt like we were in a carnival.

"You're done," the face painter said.

Bucky opened his eyes and looked at us.

"How do I look?" he said.

"You look awesome!" I said.

Hajuan and Bucky chuckled. The face painter picked up a shard that was next to him and gave it to Bucky to look at himself. He thought he did look cool.

"You should try this, Charlie," Bucky said.

I looked at Hajuan and said, "Should I?"

"Do whatever you want," Hajuan said.

At first, I wasn't sure if I was allowed to because I'm the Mindatar. But what Hajuan said, I thought, *okay, I will*. So I came and sat on the mat with the face painter in front of me. She bowed to me, and told me to close my eyes, I did just that. Then, I could feel two fingers sliding slowly on my cheeks and between my eyes.

"You're done, Mindatar," the face painter said.

I opened my eyes and picked up the shard to look at myself. I looked really cool. I had light purple markings on my cheeks and two green ones between my eyes. I looked over to Bucky and Hajuan. Bucky's eyes glowed in amazement, and Hajuan gave me two thumbs up and smiled.

I chuckled at them. I got up and noticed Ching Ching with a few other females with her on the other side of the Studio. I came to her to see what face-paint she got, Bucky and Hajuan followed. I walked to the front of her to get a closer look. She had blue droplet-like patterns on her face. I thought it was pretty on her.

Suddenly, I could hear Hajuan's heart beating quietly in his chest. I could feel how much he loves her a lot.

Bucky looked unsure if he was okay, he tapped on his leg and asked, "Hajuan? Are you okay?"

"Oh, sorry. I wasn't paying attention."

I couldn't help stop chuckling. "You're funny," I said to Hajuan.

He put one hand on the back of his head and chuckled nervously. He looked at Ching Ching who was looking at him. He stopped chuckling and his face went blue.

"Aren't you showing them around?" Ching Ching asked with a giggle.

"Right, right. I should be doing that," Hajuan said, turning to us and saying, "Let's go".

We left the Studio. I thought that was fun there, getting our faces painted for a sacred purpose. I loved it!

"What are you going to show us next?" I asked Hajuan.

He turned to me and said, "Cenote Falls."

Chapter 19

Incredible discoveries!

Hajuan took us upwards from his village and it took ten minutes walking in the wild again. I was wondering all the way what Cenote Falls would look like until we got there. Cenote Falls was a large waterfall in front of us with mossy rocks and vines. Honestly, it sort of didn't look much, until Hajuan walked straight to the waterfall. Then he turned to us and waved his hand for us to follow him. We did, but stopped in front of it. Unknowingly, Bucky and I just stood there facing in front of the fall behind Hajuan.

Hajuan was walking backwards straight to the waterfall behind him until all of a sudden, he vanished. My eyes widened in confusion, and I started chuckling nervously.

"I did *not* expect that," I said.

Suddenly, Hajuan's hand appeared from the waterfall, and he gestured to tell us to join him.

I was a little nervous about going into the waterfall. But with Bucky with me, and Hajuan to trust, I took a deep breath, grabbed Bucky's hand and we walked closer and closer to the waterfall. I looked at Bucky for a little while, then to Hajuan's hand. I reached out for it.

Hajuan grabbed mine and pulled us in. We were in the waterfall. Inside it was a glittering cave, and there was Hajuan.

"Follow me," he said, his voice echoing. We followed him deeper. I thought, while I looked around the walls, the glittering was beautiful, Bucky thought the same.

As we went deeper, we could hear something at the end of the cave. When we reached the other side, my jaw dropped in amazement, so did Bucky's.

"Wow!" Bucky shouted. There was a glowing underground river and the flora and fauna below in front of us glowed as well.

I tried to take a step towards the glittering, bioluminescent beautiful place, but Hajuan quickly grabbed my hand.

"Careful," he said, and pointed below my foot. I looked. There were purple large rocks below me leading down to the glowing river.

"Thanks for reminding me," I said. I let go of Hajuan's hand and I took a step on the rocks, but I unexpectedly slipped. I banged my face, arms, legs and hips, then eventually I splashed into the glowing river.

I swam to the surface.

"Are you alright?" Hajuan shouted from above.

I gave a thumbs up. "I'm okay!" Then I looked at the water around me and said to myself, "Bioluminescent Algae?"

Then suddenly, I heard Bucky screaming and it grew louder. As I looked, he was sliding on the slippery rocks straight towards me. I got a fright and screamed until Bucky hit the water, and splashed me. I gave him a look and Bucky looked at me.

"I'm sorry," he said.

I smiled and accepted his apology.

Unexpectedly, Hajuan came by smoothly sliding on the rocks and splashed into the water. Bucky and I got splashed.

"Oh, c'mon!" I shouted. Hajuan smiled with a snicker. Bucky nearly snickered too because of all the algae on my face. I shook my head to get rid of the algae, it all flew and landed on Hajuan and Bucky. I actually did that on purpose or for a funny reason. I start giggling.

"Got you back," I said to them.

Hajuan chuckled and wiped the algae off his face. We swam to the black bank.

We reached the bank and I noticed something glowing in the bushes. I went to investigate and noticed some movement there. I moved the leaves away to take a closer look. I gasped in amazement: a blue baby Glowtle—a glowing turtle. I picked it up and petted it, it didn't really seem to mind. I thought it was such a beautiful creature. Then more creatures emerged from the plants and saw us. They purred at us with delight. They came to us, glowing.

Some of them came to Bucky, this time he wasn't afraid. He leaned on his knees and let two glow-warming creatures cuddle him. They purred at him. Bucky really loved it, and wrapped his arms around them and brought them up to his tiny smooth slimy chest.

"Aww, they are really cute," Bucky said.

I had five creatures with me and I loved it. Hajuan had two creatures, cuddling by rubbing their tiny bodies on his feet.

I turned to him and said, "These are wonderfully beautiful creatures".

"They hide here around this glowing underground forest," he replied.

I knew that after they appeared. "You have a lucky Island," I said.

Bucky agreed.

Hajuan smiled at me. "Thank you," he said.

Then, we heard a beautiful voice that came from the glowing forest and it appeared from a tree branch. It was smaller than Bucky with beautiful sky blue eyes and a dress made of bioluma leaves. She had wings of a fairy and a headband made of small blue vines with a leaf on the top. It flew right in front of Hajuan and it looked excited to see him again.

Hajuan came closer to it and said, "Hi, Melady."

Hajuan moved his hand in front of it and it walked onto his and put its tiny hands and pressed its forehead onto his.

Bucky was amazed by the creature and came closer to them. When the creature pulled its forehead away from Hajuan's and saw Bucky, it jumped and landed its bottom on Hajuan's hand.

"Woah, it's okay, Melady. These are my friends, Bucky and Charlie. It's ok, go and see them, don't be scared, they won't hurt you."

The creature looked at him and got up. Then flapped its wings and flew right to Bucky.

Bucky didn't know what to do until Hajuan came up to him and crouched beside him.

"Here's how you do it: just move your hand below her and she'll land on it. Don't move when she's on or you'll scare her," Hajuan explained.

Bucky did that and moved his hand slowly below the creature.

It came closer and closer until she landed on his blue hand.

Bucky stared at her with curiosity even when she came closer to his face and pressed her forehead against his.

"Oof... what is it doing?" Bucky asked.

"That means she likes you, no need to be nervous, she's friendly. She does get shy around new people who enter the cave."

"Oh, she likes me?" Bucky said and the creature moved after he moved his head and landed on her bottom again in his hand.

"Careful, you almost dropped her."

"Oh! Sorry... whatever your name is."

She got back up and smiled at Bucky and Hajuan, then she flapped her wings again and flew towards Hajuan and circled him. He lifted his hand and she landed on it.

She looked at me and instead of being shy, she got excited, and flew towards me instantly. I stared at her with a smile and I lifted my hand in front of her and she landed on it.

She stared at me with a huge smile on her face.

Then she flapped her wings once again and flew around me in a playful mood.

I laughed as she circled around me like she was happy to see me for the first time.

"You look very beautiful and magical," I commented and she smiled even more.

"That's Melady, sometimes I call her the princess of Cenote Falls because she is the only one who lives here. She always wanted to see you because I told her a lot of times when you come, we would do the ceremony."

"Okay. To be honest, she has very beautiful eyes and a stunning voice."

"I agree," Bucky said. "She's so young."

"She is a young little Melafairy. I found her in this cave
when I was young. Whenever I come down to see her, she will emerge and vocalise for me, even when I play my flute."

"You have a flute?" I asked him.

"Yes I do. I bring with me wherever I go, even here. Would you like me to play it?" he asked us.

"Why not? We would like to hear you play it," I said and Bucky agreed.

Hajuan smiled and sat down with his legs crossed and took out his flute from his back. He spun it with his finger and brought the side of it to his lips and took a deep breath, then he began playing.

As he did, Melady flew on his right knee and listened to him playing.

I thought he was amazing at playing his flute and so did Bucky.

When Hajuan finished eventually, Melady looked up at him and flapped her wings and flew up beside him and gave him a tiny kiss and giggled.

Then she flew to Bucky and gave a tiny kiss too and then lastly to me and gave me a kiss.

Then she flew away and a trail of sparkly dust was left behind her.

I thought that was a beautiful moment when we met Melady and listened to Hajuan playing his flute.

Then he got up and put his flute on his back and said to both of us, "We should better leave for the village."

"Okay, Melady was very cute."

"She is when you first meet her and she always will be."

Chapter 20

The leader of the R.A.I.D

Things have completely changed for the Sorcerer. Being in the Fortress for too long? He was sick of it. He was forced to improvise, so he did. He was trying something new which was against Scarlet's rules and was also very risky: Sorcerer's joining the R.A.I.D.

He thought it was his only chance to impress the Fire Queen. Because of the Diamond Alpha, Scarlet was always fed up with flame. He headed past the Training Ground and towards the bank, and summoned three demons.

"Take me to the R.A.I.D.," he commanded them.

"Yes, master," the demons said. The demons around him grabbed his arms, and lifted him off the ground. They flew off to the R.A.I.D.

He flew almost faster than a jet and found the R.A.I.D. He flew in front of them.

The Monsters saw him and were shocked to see a Sorcerer with them.

"**What are you doing here, Jack?**" an archer shouted to him.

"I'm joining you."

"**But that's against the Queen's—**"

The Sorcerer shot a demon at him to shut him up. "No time for that. I'm in charge of the R.A.I.D now, this is how it is now. I am here to help you all. With my magic, I can help you destroy the Alpha."

The Monsters looked at each other, to see if they would either agree or not. But with the Sorcerer with magical powers, they thought it would give them the opportunity for success. They turned to their new leader and nodded to agree.

The Sorcerer raised his hand in the air and shouted, "For our Majesty!"

"For our Majesty!" The R.A.I.D shouted, raising their weapons.

Back at the Fortress, Scarlet was on her black bed looking at a frame of the Diamond Alpha and her when they were younger—a few years before Charlie became the Alpha. She sighed and frowned wryly at the picture and made her feel meh.

Suddenly, her trusted Royal Guards burst in her doors and scared her. They were puffed from running around the Fortress trying to find her. Scarlet's hair blew to flame, she grabbed a pillow, and threw it at them. The pillow hit the guard on the right.

She shouted, "Stop doing that!"

"We're sorry, your Highness. But there is something you must hear," one of them said.

"What?" she asked, glaring at them.

"You know the most trusted Sorcerer you commanded?"

"Yes. Why? What's he done?"

"Heeee... uhh... he joined the R.A.I.D".

"He what!"

Scarlet scrunched her hands and placed them on her large head and growled in frustration. "That backstabbing fool! Can you two go out for a second so I can go into a savage rage?"

They left the room for her to have her moment. They heard her raving and screaming furiously while they waited and then throwing stuff around and breaking things.

Eventually she said, "Okay, you can come back in now."

They went back in the room and they saw it was now a mess. They were about to ask her about it, but she interrupted.

"Nope. Let me speak. If anything happens to our weapon because of him, I am going to kill him!" Then she left the room. They heard her mumbling angrily until they couldn't any more.

Scarlet headed to the Dark Magic room. She walked to the cauldron and used her dark magic to control the cauldron and revealed an image of the R.A.I.D. The image showed the Sorcerer leading the R.A.I.D to find the Alpha.

116

"Oh, Jack, you better not screw this up or you will darn pay!" she said.

Chapter 21

A bad discovery

We eventually left the Underrive—it's what the underground river was called—and had the night in Hajuan's home back at the village.

I was very comfortable on the nest-like beds. It made me think like I was in my original spot back at the Alphanian Ship. Speaking of which, Bucky and I were missing our friends, and they too were missing us, a lot. We needed to head home soon. But, the Cocoanians wanted us to stay for a secret reason. I think I'd heard, when we first arrived, that they have a ceremony on a full moon. I honestly didn't know what it was for yet. But sooner or later, I would find out when a full moon rises.

The next morning arrived and I woke up. I could hear children playing and laughing and I could see them running past the doorway. I left Hajuan's home and stretched my body. I turned to my left and I saw a group of kids, Bucky was there too.

He saw me and said, "Morning, Charlie".

"Morning buddy," I replied with a smile.

Then, one of the kids came to me and asked, "Diamond Alpha? May we please show you something we found?"

"You certainly can," I said. The child grabbed my hand and took me in the small group and they showed me what they found. The objects looked very familiar. They looked like...bows. Wait a minute. They're not bows, they're crossbows!

I was terrified.

Bucky came to me and grabbed the crossbow and chucked it. "Charlie? Charlie! C'mon, Charlie! Snap out of it!" he shouted, shaking my shoulders and smacking my face. "What's wrong?"

I looked at the ground and tried to find my words, but I was too scared. Bucky put his tiny hands on my cheeks. My breath slowed down and I finally found my words, "The R.A.I.D. is coming."

Bucky dropped his hands from my cheeks and showed an alarmed look. "No, no no no! That's

119

impossible!" Then I remembered when we first met Hajuan had said when Bucky was knocked out.

"*I found a group of trespassers last night. They even had strange weapons.*"

I felt a child behind me tapping my shoulder. I turned and faced him.

"Excuse me, Diamond Alpha? What's the R.A.I.D?" the young boy asked me.

"We'll explain later. We have to warn your village!" I said. I got up and turned to the children and said, "Please, go to your families".

The children were concerned and worried, then they left for their families. I thought they were so understanding. But I didn't have enough time for second thoughts. "Come on, Bucky!" I said to Bucky.

He came and hopped on my back and I began to run. Although, it wasn't just the village we needed to warn, but also their trusted and most dependent warrior: Hajuan.

We ran around the village, trying to find Hajuan. "Hajuan! Hajuan!" we called.

We kept running and running until we found Ching Ching, we asked her where Hajuan was, she said he was in the jungle, hunting. So we went there.

We were in the jungle again, and we were urgently calling out for Hajuan. We looked around for him while we called.

"Hajuan! We need to warn you about the R.A.I.D!" I shouted.

I waited for a response, but I couldn't hear any because of Bucky's shouting. I told him to stop and he did.

We listened until we heard sounds of vines above us, we looked, it was Hajuan. He swung on the vines and slid down a tree using his spear to slow down until he touched the ground.

"Hajuan! There you are!" I said, walking to him.

"What's going on? You two sound worried," he replied.

"We came to warn you," I said.

"About what?"

"You know the group of trespassers you found a few nights ago?" I said.

"Yes, why?"

"They're coming back, worse!" I said.

Hajuan's eyes widened in shock. "How worse?"

"Worser than you can imagine! They call it the R.A.I.D" I said.

"What does that mean?" Hajuan said.

I explained what it stands for "Rampaging Army of Indestructible Doom! They're coming to wipe you all out," I said.

Hajuan looked down and took this all in, then showed a look to me, "We have to warn my village," he said.

I nodded once and said, "Let's go!"

Me, Bucky and Hajuan headed back to the village as fast as we could. We didn't know the R.A.I.D. was coming, but we had to warn the Village of Cocoa or they'd be doomed. We couldn't let that happen. We finally reached the village and headed to the centre. In the centre, there was a large rock for me to stand on, I did that and shouted, "Everyone! Please come to me!"

All the Cocoanians came from all directions straight to us.

I said to them: "We have to warn you: a reign of terror is coming! Worse than you can imagine! They're coming to wipe you all out, and take and destroy everything you love!"

The Cocoanians were terrified to hear the warning. Some were worried.

"But what are we going to do?" Ching Ching said, emerging from the Tribe with a worried look, "There will be nowhere for us to live if we lose our home."

I thought she was right, the area we were all in must've been the only place they lived, and nowhere else. I thought of another way, I looked around their homes, and found one. I knew it wasn't easy like in every battle, my only choice was to defend the island.

123

"I'll find the attackers and prevent them from reaching your home. It's…it's the only way," I said to Ching Ching.

Ching Ching was still worried, but with their beliefs and hope in me, she knew I'd protect them.

"I'm helping too," Hajuan said.

We were surprised, I thought he's got a lot of confidence and courage in him. Ching Ching burst to tears when she heard he was helping me.

She ran and hugged him, "Please, Hajuan. We don't want to lose you. You're our only warrior in our village," she said in a trembling voice.

Hajuan wrapped his arm around her while he held his spear in the other and said, "I know, Ching Ching. But it's the right thing to do. For our village."

"I'm helping too," Bucky said below me with a nervous look. I was even more surprised. Bucky just got a lot braver. And most importantly, we were a team, and we were in this together.

But before we headed back into the jungle, we needed a plan.

Chapter 22

The Sorcerer's corruption

The Sorcerer knew they were heading in the right way. He and his entire reign was ready to destroy the Diamond Alpha, and take what was valuable and treasuring.

Suddenly, he noticed purple flashes in the night sky, which meant one thing: the Corrupted Storm.

He snickered softly and said, "What I just wanted," then he smiled showing his teeth. He knew a legend about the storm: if anyone broke a legend's trust like the Fire Queen's, they would become corrupted with vengeance, darkness and the darkest magic that existed, which the Sorcerer wanted so desperately even when he had enough of Scarlet and her time-wasting tasks for him. He took a deep breath, uncrossed his arms and spaced his arms from his body and closed his eyes. Then dark magic emerged from the purple clouds and flew straight to him, circled his entire body, then painfully absorbed into his heart. He lifted his legs and curled himself because of how much pain and change was in his body. He felt himself shaking with the corruption mutating him. He started growing two more arms and two sleeves magically appeared on his robe for those arms. His veins and heart started glowing bright on his entire body until one lightning bolt struck as bright as the sun, and he finally changed form. The Sorcerer was corrupted.

The R.A.I.D had to cover their eyes during that lightning strike. They moved their arms and became shocked and some were concerned at the same time. The Sorcerer was hovering above them using no demons, facing the R.A.I.D. with his eyes shut. He opened his eyes; they were now glowing purple and his pupils were a pinkish red.

"He's done it," one of the Monsters in the R.A.I.D said.

"Rise my people! Rise and now call me: the Corrupted Sorcerer!" he shouted. More lightning struck on the sea and the Corrupted Sorcerer's laugh was sinister.

Chapter 23

The plan

We could hear loud violent thunderstorms out on the ocean's horizon, I knew they were closing in. We quickly made a plan for what to do: I would draw the R.A.I.D. in the jungle to an open space we found, and when they were in the spot we wanted them in, I would give the signal to fight.

As the R.A.I.D. got closer, I noticed an unusual thing hovering above the water with the storms following. I squinted to get a closer look at it, then to the storms. The R.A.I.D. got closer and I noticed something bad! They never sent Sorcerers because it was against my Nemesis's rules. This Sorcerer broke her trust and got corrupted! *This is going to be challenging*, I thought, but this was the only way to protect the village.

"Positions," I said to Hajuan and Bucky.

Bucky climbed on Hajuan's back and Hajuan slid down the tree we were on, and they went to their positions that were hidden. I went to the ground.

I looked at Hajuan and Bucky.

"Good luck, Charlie," Hajuan said.

"Be careful, Charlie," Bucky said, looking worried.

I nodded at them, "For the Village of Cocoa," I said to both of them, and they said the same. I took out my Diamond Rapier and showed a ready look to the darkness and ran straight into it.

I kept my eyes and ears peeled for any sign of the R.A.I.D. I felt a little nervous about them being anywhere near me and getting me. I walked alone in the darkness for a little while until I heard voices nearby. I came to investigate, but kept my distance. It was the R.A.I.D. bringing their boats up to the sand, I noticed the cursed Sorcerer hovering on the sand. I noticed the veins in his arms, I thought it was a little bit creepy.

"What next, Corrupted Sorcerer?" one of the archers asked. I thought the name was unusual, 'Corrupted Sorcerer'. I listened.

"We will first track down the Diamond Alpha, and capture her and her sidekick. Then, we'll scatter around the island and take what will be ours. We will even kill what took down the group," the Corrupted Sorcerer said. I was alarmed by that, he meant they were going to kill Hajuan!

I don't think so! I thought. I looked at them and shouted, "Hey! Over here!"

The Corrupted Sorcerer saw me, "The Diamond Alpha!" he shouted, his glowing eyes widened.

The others looked over and saw me, and raised their weapons.

"After her!" The Corrupted Sorcerer shouted, the Monsters started coming for me,

"Oh crud!" I said, and started running back into the jungle with the Monsters on my tail.

I ran back into the jungle with the Monsters chasing me, which was part of the plan. They shot arrows at me, I outmanoeuvred them. I looked behind, there was something even worse than the arrows: the Corrupted Sorcerer was there, hovering above the ground. The veins in his arms glowed to his hands, and he began shooting pink lightning at me. That was a challenge to outmanoeuvre, but I successfully did.

The Corrupted Sorcerer growled in annoyance, I sighed in relief, but not for long. I looked in front of me, there was a large ravine in front of me. I screamed.

I looked behind and I knew there would be no way past them, the ravine was getting closer and closer. I took a deep breath and took a leap of faith, over the ravine I went. I made it and kept running. I looked back and the Monsters stopped at the ravine, except the Corrupted Sorcerer.

That wasn't part of the plan, but it was too late, I kept running with the Corrupted Sorcerer behind me. I avoided multiple obstacles in front of me while the Corrupted Sorcerer kept shooting lightning at me. Then I finally reached the space where Bucky and Hajuan were waiting and I shouted, "*Now!*"

Chapter 24

The fight against the Corrupted Sorcerer

Hajuan and Bucky jumped out from their spots and Hajuan gave the Corrupted Sorcerer a real blow from his fist. Bucky came out from the other side with a large branch as a weapon, whacking the Corrupted Sorcerer on the gut as hard as he could.

The Corrupted Sorcerer flew uncontrollably to the air until he controlled himself. He looked at us. I took out my Diamond Rapier and gave him my battle expression. Bucky and Hajuan did the same. The Corrupted Sorcerer snickered and said, "You fools," and called to the clouds using his bare hands.

The lightning struck his hands and then he shot a strong lightning strike at us, and we jumped out of the way just in time before the strike hit us. The storms above us got more violent than they were before. I had to find a way to make it easier for us to get him. I looked around, from the trees, ground, Bucky then finally to Hajuan.

I had an idea. I said to Hajuan, "Hajuan, can you throw me up to him?"

He looked at me, thinking if I was crazy. But then I said, "Trust me: I can make it easier when he's lowered." He looked in one direction, then looked at me and nodded. We grabbed each of our forearms and started spinning each other. Then we let go of each other when we fast enough. I flew to the air and straight to the Corrupted Sorcerer, I shot myself upside down and kicked him hard. He hit the ground.

Hajuan came and placed his spear on the Corrupted Sorcerer's neck to prevent him from getting up. I dropped to the ground on my feet, came to the Corrupted Sorcerer and said, "It's over, Corrupted Sorcerer," Bucky agreed, crossing his arms. The Corrupted Sorcerer noticed Hajuan's tattoo on his hand and his eyes widened. Then, he showed an angry look to Hajuan and shouted, "You!".

The Corrupted Sorcerer used his power and strongly pushed us away. Hajuan flew in the air and hit a stone wall behind him, and fell to the ground. Then he used his power and grabbed him and hit him hard on a large rock and it broke to pieces.

"Hajuan!" I shouted, I ran to him, but I was caught by the power of the Corrupted Sorcerer, and he held me tight. I was unable to move.

"Charlie! Hajuan!" Bucky shouted, terrified and trying to hide, but he got caught too. The Corrupted Sorcerer both held us tight, and hovered over to Hajuan, who was injured badly.

"You did it," the Corrupted Sorcerer sneered angrily at Hajuan.

"Did what?" Hajuan said, grunting in pain,

"You killed the group the Queen sent," the Corrupted Sorcerer answered aggressively.

"I was protecting my village," Hajuan shouted, the Corrupted Sorcerer grabbed him by his neck with two of his left arms and lifted him up in the air.

"This is pathetic! Now, it is time you die."

I watched as the Corrupted Sorcerer lifted Hajuan in the air. Hajuan looked really hurt, he had a purple eye and lots of bruises, scratches and cuts. My eyes widened, terrified. I was about to cry with fear. But instead, I felt angry, *very* angry! Because I'm the Mindatar, I have an ultimate weapon: my anger.

I shut my eyes and started trying to break the magic that held me and Bucky tight by spreading my body apart. I growled heavily as I did. I got stronger and stronger than I usually was.

"Hey!" I shouted to the Corrupted Sorcerer, he looked at me and his eyes widened with fear, "How about you, leave…him…ALONE!"

The Corrupted Sorcerer dropped Hajuan to the ground, and helplessly watched me. I got stronger and stronger until I broke free and released a bright flash of light.

I opened my glowing eyes, and dashed towards the Corrupted Sorcerer and started beating his chest, stomach and back. He flew backwards and I did not give him any chances, I just straight kept coming for him and kept bashing him. Then I threw him into the air, and I jumped up to him, and punched him harder to the ground. Then I grabbed his feet and started spinning him faster and faster, until I let go. I watched him as he screamed into the air until he disappeared into the horizon of the ocean. My breathing was rough until I started slowly breathing and calming my temper, and my eyes changed back to my original colour.

The dark magic disappeared and Bucky was free. He ran towards me and hugged me, and started laughing in excitement.

"Charlie! We did it!" Bucky shouted gleefully.

I chuckled exhaustingly. "We did."

Then I looked at Hajuan, who was still on the ground, heavily breathing and grunting in pain. Bucky and I went to him.

"Hajuan. Are you okay?" I asked him.

"My...my arm's broken," Hajuan said weakly, grunting in pain.

"Here, we'll help you up," I said.

We helped Hajuan up and headed to the village once more.

Chapter 25

Defeat for the R.A.I.D

The R.A.I.D was still behind after the Diamond Alpha escaped with their new leader, and the ravine was way too big to cross. They were forced to turn back. But then it became urgent because they suddenly heard their leader screaming from above. The Diamond Alpha must've beaten him!

"*Retreat!*" One of them shouted in fear, they ran away from the ravine and straight back to their boats. They began rowing away from the island in fear and into the horizon. The Corrupted Clouds started to clear away, revealing the stars and the Silver Moon.

Meanwhile, the Corrupted Sorcerer flew uncontrollably in the air, faster than a plane, and all the way back to the mainland. He painfully slid onto the grass. Eventually he stopped. But sadly for him, the corruption began to wear off and he was back to normal. His two arms were gone and the pattern on his forehead was gone. His dark robe stayed the same however. His eyes changed back to his original, and the dark magic was gone. He didn't know that part of the old legend unfortunately.

He lifted his head off the ground and groaned with pain. He shook his head because he was dizzy. Suddenly, he noticed a familiar shadow that looked like the Diamond Alpha's, but it was even worse. He looked up, it was Scarlet with her hair blowing red.

The Sorcerer chuckled nervously, "Your... Highness?"

"You betrayed me!" Scarlet said angrily.

"Your Highness, please, I-I can explain," the Sorcerer prayed, but he got cut off.

"No time for explanation, Jack! You are going to pay for this! Leaving me here and making me do everything *for* you, and breaking *my* trust?!" she shouted angrily to him as the Sorcerer whimpered helplessly. "This is all *your* fault, Jack. Calling yourself the Corrupted Sorcerer? It sounds pretty cool, but breaking my rules? *My rules*?" she shouted.

"Your Highness, please, please give me a chance".

"That was your chance, Jack. Now it's game over for you!" she said, getting angrier and angrier.

"*What is wrong with you*?" Her body began to burn.

"Look, I'm sorry, your Majesty. I thought this was the only way to make you happy—".

"*That was a rhetorical question!*" She shouted even more angrily. Then she started screaming dramatically and her entire body turned to savage flames.

"Oh no!" the Sorcerer whimpered.

Scarlet made a huge flaming explosion that was heard in Pollen Village. The villagers there heard it.

"Farmer Brenda? Did you hear that?" The blacksmith said to Farmer Brenda.

"I did, Bruce. The Fire Queen must be very angry," Farmer Brenda said.

"Well, she does do that. Did you hear that the Diamond Alpha went to the East to explore?" Bruce asked.

"I did. I hope she's okay," she said.

"She's immortal," Bruce said.

"Ah, yes, yes. She is, you're right. Good point," she said, and continued harvesting her crop farm.

Chapter 26

The return to the Village of Cocoa

It was a day's journey back to Hajuan's village and it just reached morning. We were exhausted from the fight and we were proud that we saved the island together. Even though all battles are hard and we get lots and injuries, Hajuan was still sore, but luckily he started healing up and limping less.

Eventually, we finally came back to the Village of Cocoa, and all the Cocoanians were cheering for us. I felt more proud of myself too and of my friends, Bucky and Hajuan. Bucky was excited about all the cheering and smiles from the Tribe. Hajuan was looking around the crowd for Ching Ching, because he wanted to see her.

"Where's Ching Ching?" he asked the Tribe. They cleared their way to show Ching Ching.

"Ching Ching," he said with a happy smile.

"Hajuan!" she shouted to him. She ran and hugged him.

"Whoa, careful, Ching Ching. My-my arm's broken," he reminded her.

"Oh… sorry. I just- I…" She struggled to find her words.

Hajuan waited for what she would say. That reminded me of when I struggled to find my words back home. Thankfully, Stephenie helped me by telling me to breathe. So I did the exact same thing for Ching Ching: I silently told her to breathe.

Ching Ching nodded at me and took three slow deep breaths, eventually she smiled.

"I love you, Hajuan" She finally found her words.

Hajuan had a huge smile on his face. Then Ching Ching wrapped her arms around Hajuan's neck and pressed her lips against his. I thought that was romantic. Bucky watched too. Hajuan was happy to be home with his special girl. When they finished, I continued helping Hajuan move towards his home, and we went inside.

We helped Hajuan onto his nest-like bed and I told Bucky to stay with him when I was going to go out to find large leaves to make a green bandage like Hajuan did. But instead, I noticed his neck wrap and I thought it would come in handy.

I went back in and asked him for his neck wrap, he took it off with his unbroken arm and gave it to me. I carefully wrapped it around his broken arm and then looped it under his head.

He looked at me with a smile and said, "Thank you".

"Anytime, Hajuan," I replied with a smile.

Hajuan looked around for a little while then said with a smile, "You and Bucky are the coolest friends I've met."

Bucky and I looked at each other smiling,

"We are?" Bucky said with a happy smile. I chuckled at him. Then I looked back at Hajuan.

"You should get some rest," I said to him.

"I'll be fine, Charlie. Tonight, there is one more thing we must show you both," Hajuan said.

Bucky and I got excited about that. I already knew he wouldn't spoil it, so we didn't this time.

"Okay, we'll be patient this time," I said.

As time passed and the sun began to set, I actually wanted it to because Bucky and I wanted to see the last surprise. Hajuan must've been full of surprises lately. Like I said before the Droplet Tree, I even hoped that this one was mind-blowing.

Right now, Bucky and I were watching the stars. We even chatted about all the fun we'd had with Hajuan and the village. Speaking of Hajuan, I checked on him a few times in the morning, and he was healing up while he rested. I was hoping he would be alright, because the Corrupted Sorcerer damaged him pretty darn much.

Bucky found a shooting star and said, "A shooting star! Make a wish."

I held my wish for a sec, and thought of our friends back home in the Oceanic Mountainside. I hoped they were watching the night sky too. I felt a tear on my cheek because I missed them, so I wished I could see them again.

Then, we heard footsteps coming to us, and noticed a familiar shadow. We looked, it was Hajuan holding his spear, smiling at us. He looked much better. There were no bruises, cuts, scratches or black eyes anymore, but he still had the bandage on his right arm.

"Ready for the surprise?" he asked us, and we nodded excitedly.

"C'mon," he said. We got up and followed him.

"You're looking much better now. No more bruises or cuts and your black eye is gone, but I hope your arm will be okay," I said.

He looked at me and smiled. "My arm will be okay".

Chapter 27

The sacred ceremony

We headed back to the village, and for some reason, the female Cocoanians were dressed as beautiful aqua dancers. They wore traditional half-clothing patterned with water drops and bubbles and their threaded skirts were as blue as blueberries. They even wore small blue orchid crowns. I thought that was just incredible, the females wearing those kinds of traditional clothing. We then started walking into the wild again.

I was looking around the passing surroundings, Bucky was doing the same thing next to me. We found a few glowing creatures emerging, and they watched us as we passed them. We kept walking, and walking, and walking until I felt a drop land on my head.

"What the—" I said. I looked up, then my eyes widened. There was a large familiar black tree, and we were walking straight to it.

"The Droplet Tree?" Bucky said.

Hajuan and the females nodded. "I didn't tell you both this because I wanted to keep it a surprise: the Droplet Tree holds an ancient secret," he answered.

I looked at Hajuan, and I asked, "What's the ancient secret?"

"Follow us, and we'll show you," he answered. We continued following them closer and closer to the Droplet Tree. We found an entrance and went inside.

We passed the wooden roots inside the Droplet Tree until we were in the centre. Then, Bucky and I saw something amazing: a shrine!

"A shrine?" Bucky shouted in amazement.

"Wow!" I shouted.

"The Water Shrine has been waiting for you, Charlie, that was why we waited for you," Hajuan said.

I came to the shrine to get a closer look at it. *It looks incredibly ancient,* I thought. Then, I found a picture of myself on the stone wall and noticed

Mindoglyphics that were reading: 'The Mindatar is the one to command the sea.'

I didn't really get that yet.

Then Ching Ching came to me and said, "Please lie on the Aqua circle."

I went to the Aqua circle in the centre, and lay down.

They told me to close my eyes, and I did that. I believed something was just beginning.

"What are they doing to Charlie?" I heard Bucky ask.

I couldn't hear Hajuan's voice because of the females singing.

Then, I felt like I was dreaming, I couldn't feel anything else, I felt like I was floating. Then, I felt a liquidy thing touching my feet, and then my entire body; It was like sleeping underwater. Then, my head felt awake, and I opened my eyes. They shone bright as stars.

Eventually, I slowly hovered to the ground on top of my unsteady legs. Bucky came to me, so did Hajuan. I felt soggy.

"Charlie?" Bucky softly said.

I opened my eyes.

"Charlie!" Bucky shouted gleefully, and hugged me.

I hugged him. I looked at Hajuan. "What just happened?" I asked him.

"This was a ceremony for you. You can command the sea," Hajuan answered.

"But I thought I already could because I'm the Mindatar," I said.

"You're a novice Mindatar," Hajuan answered.

That made sense, because I was a novice. "You have a point," I said.

"C'mon, we should head back to the village," Hajuan said to us and the females, and then we left the shrine, out of the Droplet Tree and back to the Village of Cocoa.

Chapter 28

The journey home begins

We had the final night at the village, now it was for us time to say goodbye. My heart wanted to stay, but we needed to head home to see our friends again. Me, Bucky and the Tribe headed to the shore where we were swept up.

Their children were sad for us to go. They came to us and one said, "Will you please stay with us? Please?"

I crouched down to them and said softly, "I know you're sad, but we can still visit you all, every month we will."

That cheered them up, they smiled and cuddled me. I liked them cuddling me, I thought it was cute. Then they came and cuddled Bucky, I thought that was cuter.

I looked at Hajuan and Ching Ching who were standing next to each other, holding their hands.

Hajuan came to me and said thankfully, "Thank you for coming to us," he said, and the others nodded.

"No problem," I said, smiling. I turned to the sea, and went closer until the water was touching my feet.

"Let me teach you something," Hajuan said, coming to me. He grabbed my hand and placed the tip of my hand in my mouth. He told me to whistle, so I whistled as hard as I could, then we waited for a response. Suddenly, we heard a large roar from the sea, and a large red fin appeared on the surface: a Long-Finned Leviathan.

Bucky and I nearly panicked as the Leviathan came closer until it touched the sand in the water. Then, I remembered a thing of what Hajuan said when we first met: "They were probably happy to see you".

I took a deep breath and bravely went closer to the Leviathan. I slowly and bravely reached my hand between the eyes of the Monster, and looked away. I felt it touch my hand and purr.

I looked at it, surprised, Hajuan was right: they were happy to see me. I put my other hand on the beautiful creature and smiled. I thought they were dangerous to everyone, but now I understood they don't attack me or anyone who lives above or in their territory. They only attacked trespassers that were in smaller groups. But they'll never attack me or my Alphanians.

The Leviathan showed its long tail for me and Bucky to climb on. Before we did, I turned to everyone watching us and smiling. I came to them and said goodbye. I faced Hajuan and said, "I hope your arm will be okay."

Hajuan chuckled. "Thanks, Charlie," he said, and hit the side of his chest twice.

I did the same for him. Then we could hear Bucky sobbing.

"Are you crying, Bucky?" Ching Ching asked him.

"No," Bucky said with a sniff. Ching Ching chuckled and gave him a hug, he needed one.

Then the children came and hugged him, they must've really liked him I thought.

Hajuan and I watched Ching Ching and the children as they cuddled Bucky until Bucky felt better. Then I felt Hajuan put his hand on my shoulder blade and said, "Goodbye, Charlie".

"Goodbye, Hajuan," I said. Then the children and Ching Ching let Bucky come and he climbed on my leg and on to my head. Then I headed to the Long-Finned Leviathan, and turned to the Tribe for the second last time. Then I climbed onto the Leviathan's head, and the Leviathan turned and swam away from the island. The Tribe waved to us as they shrunk in the horizon. We waved back at them until we couldn't see them anymore. The journey home had begun!

Chapter 29

A song for Bucky and the night

The Leviathan swam with us on its head, even when night hit. We watched the constellations above, and remembered all the fun we had with Hajuan and the Tribe. It was really quiet that night, though; there wasn't really much for us to do. We started feeling bored.

Then I first thought of having a chat, I turned to Bucky and asked, "Are you looking forward to seeing our friends again?"

Bucky looked at me and nodded, and sighed deeply. I looked to the scales of the Leviathan, and tried to think of something else. I had an idea.

I turned to Bucky and said, "Would you like to listen to music?"

He looked at me, confused. "We don't have music, Charlie."

"No, Bucky, I meant this". I smacked my legs to make a melody, but Bucky was still confused.

155

I tried to make him understand what I meant, but eventually he said, "It's alright, Charlie".

Then he faced down to the scales. I sighed, but then I thought of doing it. I took a deep breath, and began patting my belly and my legs, and clapping.

Bucky looked at me and asked, "What are you doing?"

"Doing a song I listened to in the human world: the Cup Song," I answered, and continued on.

As I smacked and clapped, Bucky smiled and enjoyed listening to me as I smacked and clapped, smacked and clapped. I wanted to do it for Bucky and the night. When I finished, Bucky was lying down next to me, dreaming with a smile. I felt tired too, so I laid down comfortably next to him and looked at the stars, then I rested my eyes.

I was really excited when we saw our friends again. It has been days or a week or two that we haven't seen them, but we'd be thrilled to see them again.

Chapter 30

Home at last!

I was very comfy on the smooth scales of the Leviathan, and again, I could see the orange light from inside my eyes. I could feel Bucky on me, and I knew that we're still moving on the water. The Leviathan, I was guessing, just never gave up. Besides, I was dreaming of when we saw our friends again.

I felt Bucky getting up. I heard nothing but the sloshes of water. I honestly didn't want to get up because I was so wrapped up in sleeping until I heard him gasp and yelled in excitement.

I quickly woke up. "W…wha… what's going on?" I said, fatigued.

"Look!" Bucky shouted, and pointed to something in the distance.

I looked, and gasped excitedly.

The Oceanic Mountainside!

We were finally home!

Bucky jumped while shouting continuously, "Home! Home! Home!"

I got up and watched the Oceanic Mountainside get closer and closer. We saw the Alphanian Ship, but none of our friends appeared yet.

The Leviathan reached the green shore, and we climbed off. I looked around the green glades, and then to the ship. We were really excited to be back.

I turned around to the Leviathan and said, "Thank you". The Leviathan purred at me, then we watched as it dived back into the sea.

Eventually we turned back around to the Alphanian Ship. I was about to touch my Amulet, but I stopped for a moment and I turned to the ocean horizon.

I watched it, because I was thinking if the Cocoanians, I was sure they missed us already, but I promised them that we would come back. I smiled to the horizon, and hit my chest twice again like Hajuan did. Then I turned back to the

Alphanian Ship, touched my Amulet and said, "Everyone, we're finally home!"

We waited for our friend's reply, but nothing. Our smiles began to fade, and we looked to the ground, feeling sad. I made a long sigh of depression until suddenly we heard a squeal of excitement coming from the Alphanian Ship. We looked and saw Violet!

Our smiles were restored, and we waved to her excitedly. She waved back, then went inside to tell the others. We came to the side of the ship, and waited. Then, we saw our eight friends above and they jumped down to us and started hugging us in delight and laughter.

We were so happy to see each other again, very happy. They were saying to us, "Where did you get those cool face markings?" Tar asked.

"Are you okay?"

"We're so happy to see you again!"

"What did you find?"

Bucky and I told them the fun discoveries. Then, after hugging seven of them, me and Bucky

159

were up to Chuckboi and saw that he had a huge smile on his face. He wrapped me with his prehensile tail and grabbed Bucky and squeezed us like he missed us more.

"I'm so happy you two came back!" he said.

"Yeah, we protect each other, good thing I'm immortal," I said in a cramped voice. He put us down eventually.

Stephenie came to us and said, "You know, after you guys were gone, we came to Pollen Village, and told the Villagers about it. One day I went to the village alone, and discovered some were putting up papers saying, 'Diamond Alpha heads to the East'," she said.

I chuckled. "They're probably just jealous of my immortality."

Bucky agreed.

Stephenie thought that too, and thought I was right.

"And about that, we should head to the village and tell them you two are back," Violet said, and we all agreed.

160

"That's a good idea," I said, then we headed to the village. I was really happy to be home, but I would still go back to the Tribe, maybe bring our friends along, they'd appreciate it. I believed they would even show us more secrets in the future.

The End

**Book 2: IMAGINE
The Long Winter**
Coming soon
Pre-order here:
https://www.annieseaton.net/store.html